Return To Limestone ...

... Where Your Vacation Dreams Come True!

By

Deborah Bartlow Tackett

Tackett Publications
P.O. Box 379
Arkadelphia, AR 71923

397/500

Copyright 1998

By

Deborah Bartlow Tackett

Deborah Tackett grew up in Indianapolis, Indiana. She now lives in Arkadelphia, Arkansas with her husband and daughter. She and her husband operate an insurance agency. *Return to Limestone* is her first story.

Dedication

This book is dedicated to my parents, who are always supportive of me. Thank you for providing me with the opportunities to really experience life.

In memory of Grandma Gracie, whose love I cherish and whose special memories are imprinted on my heart forever.

To my daughter, Adrienne. I hope this diary helps explain a little more of who I am. I love you so very much.

Special thanks to Pat Adcock and Beverly Slavins for their help editing and their thoughtful comments.

To my wonderful husband, John, my mentor and friend. I appreciate his sketches and am so grateful for his constant motivation. Without his support this book would not have been completed. Now that I have shared the places, described within these pages, with him, let's "Return to Limestone."

Table of Contents

Contributing Players 7

Foreword 9

Chapters

The Dream 11
The Honeymoon 22
Cabin #5 26
Climate and Terrain 28
Winter in the U.P. 32
The People 33
The Moral 35
The Quest for a Simpler Life 37
Life in the U.P. 43
The Other Cabins   Cabin #1 43
                     Cabin #2 44
                     Cabins #3 and #4 47
The Incident 49
My First Trip Alone 54
I Thought Matt Would Never Leave 55
Grandma's House 58
The Trailer 62
Navigating the AuTrain 64
The Smells at Grandma's 66
My Friend, Rachel Bennett, and Her Poetry 68
Summer of the Turtle 70
The Brissons   Vic and Emma 72
                Mary and Barbie 74

Limestone 76
Old Joe's 78
Beer 81
Chores at the Lake 83
My Mud Puppy 85
Learning to Swim 86
Charlie the Snake 87
And They Came 88
       Howard Parr 89
       John Bergquest 89
       Louie Johnson 90
       Louie's Family 92
My First Airplane Ride 93
The Storm 94
Nature's Playground 95
Chatham 100
The Food Up North 101
Trenary 103
Traunik 108
Munising 111
Christmas 114
Reflection 117

Appendix 119

I have so many special memories of my summers in Limestone. These memories are made possible by my special relationships with the locals and our guests. All of these people, and many I do not recall by name, held a special place in Grandma's heart.

Harry and Betty Allison, Indianapolis, IN

Lillian and Harold Anttila, Limestone Post Office

Rachel Bennett, friend

John Bergquist, neighbor, Limestone, MI

Leslie and Ethel Birk, the helpers

Joe Braun, caretaker ($100 month)

Evangeline "Vangie" Bresaue, Louie's mother

Buz, Mary and Barbie Brisson, Limestone, MI

Vic and Emma Brisson, neighbors, Limestone, MI

Jim Coffman, Indianapolis, IN

John and Sue Coltharp, Brazil, IN

George "Snowball" Cummings, the postman

Patsy and Bob Dierdorf, Grace's brother, Brazil, IN

Jim and Edyth Dierdorf, Grace's parents, Brazil, IN

Dot and Murt (the sisters)

Francis and Herb Finlan, Herb's Tavern and Trenary Store

Jack Garber, Grandma's friend

Cecil, Helen and Steve Holt, Minooka, IL

Bob and Mary Grace Hunt, cousins, Brazil, IN

Junior Johnson's trailer beside Tom Roy's A-frame

Louie Johnson, Grandma's soul mate

Jerome Johnson, Louie's son

Evelyn Korhonen, Louie's sister and Jeanette's mom

Jay, Dorothy and Rick Miller, Plainfield, IN

Howard Parr, tree cutter

Shirley and Larry Paullus, cousins, Brazil, IN

Ray and Jeanette Radovich, Louie's niece

Fred Rowcliff, Batavia, IL (bought Cabin #4)

Pug and Norm Roy, Limestone, MI

Leroy and Mary Schepper, Grace's sister, Brazil, IN

Matt Telliga, Flint, MI

Ron, Cecelia, Jennifer, John, Bethany and Brent Testy

Tinny, the butcher

Pearl Tweedal, Norm Roy's sister

Bob and Louise Vollmer, friends

Bill and Mable Wyatt, Indianapolis, IN

Foreword

Grandpa Paul's life affected many others; not just its existence, but the lack thereof, upon his death. Grandpa was ordinary, except that he was a man with a dream and like few other people in this world, he fulfilled his. I have only select specific memories of him.

Perhaps my most vivid memory was when I was only seven years old. Unfortunately, I remember my dad receiving a phone call in the middle of the night. Grandpa had passed away. It was March 26, 1968.

Grandma had befriended several local ladies and this had been their bowling night. They nicknamed her "Gutter Gracie." She returned home and found Grandpa lying beside the bed with one sock in his hand. He had slipped away quickly and quietly while getting ready for bed.

Perhaps not until I began my "Michigan" journal did I realize the eventual shaping of my life did not begin until the finality of another. When a life ends another begins...and so it was with mine. At only seven years of age I had an entire lifetime ahead of me. It was probably because of his death that Grandma began asking me to spend my summers with her in Michigan. The experiences that follow are what shaped my life.

Events began to develop in 1947 that would have decades of consequences. These eventual consequences would span families and generations, the fallout of which is yet unpredicted 50 years later.

With a diligent effort to be as factual as possible and to preserve my memories this narrative acts as a diary and mode of entertainment. With my Grandmother's guidance through letters, bookkeeping logs, her phone books, pictures and general ledger, dated 1958-1977 I attempt to compile my *Return to Limestone.*

Please join me as I begin my journey to preserve this slice of life, the feelings, sights and sounds that have been preserved and imprinted on my memory. They are so plentiful I don't know where to begin, except perhaps with the obvious — the dream.

The Dream

Goose bumps rise on her spindly legs. The fragrance of pine and recently mown grass was light in the morning air after the light rain shower. The crisp summer breeze off the lake made wisps of fine brown hair tickle her cheek much like a grand daddy long leg walking through the fine hairs on her forearm. Her heavy eyelids barely open and she decides not to swat herself.

The feeling was carefree — not lazy, but intentionally laid back. It was as if time stood still on this Northern paradise.

Paul Munier and Harry Allison

Nothing was urgent. The music of frogs and seagulls joined in with the melodious rustle of the maple and the slow lapping of the tide on the water's edge. Have I been asleep? What time is it or does it really matter?

It is now clear to me why my Grandma Gracie, Grandpa Paul and their son/my dad, Dick, changed their annual vacation destination to the Au Train Basin in Limestone, Michigan — the serenity, simplistic beauty and loving people of the area.

Their previous vacations had been to Minnesota's Butcher Cabins on Lost Lake, then they were told of a new resort just south of Munising, Michigan. Their treks to the Upper Peninsula (U.P.) began a lifetime of family excursions to this beautiful unspoiled wilderness. The U.P. has 4,300 inland lakes and is surrounded by three of the Great Lakes.

When the pressures of city life and work became almost too much for Grandpa they decided to take a six month reprieve from work. In 1959 they escaped to the Au Train Basin. This time and place of healing convinced Grace and Paul that, following retirement, this was where they wanted to spend the remainder of their lives. This would not just be a summer retreat but would become their home.

Their journey was an effort to escape the complexities of "city" life, in Indianapolis, Indiana. Their love for the place and desire to retire there someday motivated them to save every penny they could muster and begin purchasing:

* Five cabins, from Herb Finlan, in 1956.

They purchased these with Grace's sister, Mary and her husband, Leroy Schepper. They were to be partners only a short time, for when Paul and Grace decided to retire in Michigan, they bought the other half of the partnership from Leroy and Mary.

* A 1957, 8' by 36', Buddy trailer (Model 36D, Serial # 361024) out of which business was conducted.

They purchased this from E.J. Kucela for $2622 including interest and moving expense and paid it off in 1962.

* 40 acres of land on which Cabin #1 was located.

The other four cabins rested in Section 24 on land owned by Cleveland Cliffs, an iron ore company. Cleveland Cliffs owned the Au Train River Basin and much of the surrounding land. They contracted a 100-year lease. It began at $150 annual payment from 1/1/59 to 1/1/60. After that it was raised to $250 a year.

* and, another 40 acres of land complete with a one bedroom, white frame house, on Highway 67.

It is located, as are the cabins, in the Hiawatha National Forest. The house, per the Alger County Plat Book rests in Limestone Township 4N, Range 21W, Section 34. This three room house later become Grandma and Grandpa's home.

Leslie Birk helped Grandpa add on to the house. They built a bi-level living room, complete with fireplace and large attached garage. This much needed addition allowed the previous living room to function as the second bedroom. The addition changed the appearance of the small house into a very comfortable retirement home.

Finally, in 1967, Paul completed 35 years at Link Belt. Grace's career included employment at Indiana State Teachers Association, a life insurance company and, finally, twelve years at United Auto Workers (UAW).

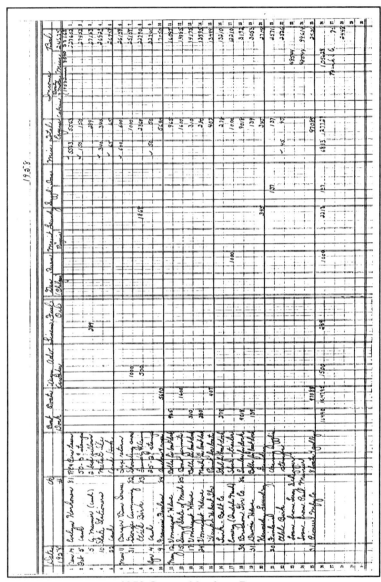

1958 General Ledger Page

Four of the five cabins that Grace and Paul purchased were situated on the Au Train Basin. Au Train Basin, "the lake" as the locals call it, is approximately seven miles long and one-half mile wide. Cabin #1 was located about a half mile up the hill.

Those born since the 1970's, the time of the Holiday Inn's, will find it hard to imagine a "resort" just a notch above tent camping and camper trailers. Imagine actually paying to stay in a place where people brave the cold, insects and have no running water, indoor bathrooms or electricity.

From town only the last four digits of the phone number needed to be dialed for local calls. There were so few people, there was no need to dial the prefix. Perhaps some today would call it quaint. I do know one thing, I'd definitely be lost without my blow dryer and curling iron. I know, Dad, you had to walk five miles to school and back going uphill both ways...

They advertised in the following publications:

Grand Rapids Press, Indianapolis Star, Indianapolis Times, Terre Haute Star, Milwaukee Journal, Outdoor Life and Yukon Sportsman magazines.

Their advertisement read something like this:

Cabins for Rent

Your choice of five cabins. Four located on the Au Train Basin. Available Memorial weekend through October. Weekly rates from $30-60. Gas kitchens, fully furnished. Great fishing and hunting. Boat and motor rental available.

Please call (317) 839-0260 or write: Paul and Grace Paul Munier, 9848 Bradbury Drive, Indianapolis, Indiana 46231 or Box No. 3, Limestone, Michigan.

1971

Date 1971	A/c #	Explanation	Adv	Sup Gl	Equip Baitshop	Bar Baitshop	Fire	Laundry Lerang	Maint Boats	Maint Other	Misc	Stat Gl	Supp Gl	Exp Gl	Total Exp	Cabins	B+M Grocery	Sto Gl
Mar 2	401	Howard Parr — shoveling snow										2100			1000			
Apr 3	402	George Buw — Dear	23.39								12.00				1800			220.00
Apr 16	403	L D Allen — 25.00 mattress									11.00				2234			
May 30	404	Howard Parr — cutting wood & boats								1100	31.50				1100			
May 31	409	Pat O'Connell — cleaning								3150	31.00				3150			
	410	Pat O'Connell — cleaning								3000					3000			
15		Chatham Shop — cleaning											843		843			
26		Bennie O'Connell — Cabin 3 Prems — Mary								2170					2170			
			23.39							2170 104.30	24.50 12.00		843		14703	3600 3600		
July 11	411	Howard Parr — mowing & boats								1000					1000			
9	412	Limestone O.O — staining										1400			1400			
10	413	Whitestone Shakga — 210 qts													3340			
11	414	Richwood Gl — paid gl		32.68	33.40						3947			3947	6217			
23	415	Argyle Stor — Ot — 3 dzns													749			
17	416	Jack Knew — Ins — Lilidor	7.92			31.25.17									2125			
18		Argyle — sink — gar								1327					1357			
29		Savage — Multi gar Phone 407 Shop 1.80						354			497	180	337		354 10114			
21		Pat O'Connell — cleaning								1150					1150			
22		Jim Jauch — cleaning								6000					6000			
24		Whitestone Shakga — 1½ mantles								681			687		687			
		juna																1115
			7.92	32.68	33.40	21/25.20			354	9477	497	1580	1024	3949	259406	35100	14050	

HUNT   FISH   RELAX

AuTrain Basin Cabins

A View Of The Lake From The Cabins

In the Hiawatha National Forest, Alger County, in Michigan's Beautiful Upper Peninsula.

When you think of going on vacation, you get the idea you want to "get away from it all" for awhile—don't you? Here you can "hide-away" and do pretty much as you please—hunt, fish, swim, go hiking, take scenic trips or just "loaf."

Where Your Vacation Dreams Come True

Down the Lane to AuTrain Basin Cabins

COME AND FISH . . . . for the REST of your life!

The lake is approximately 10 miles long and ½ mile wide. There are tree stumps scattered over the lake, log and driftwood jams along the outer edges where big bass (up to 7½ pounds) are always waiting to break your line—several islands scattered over the lake—really a BASS HEAVEN.

Paul Decker of Mishawaka, Indiana, and his fishing buddies always get their limit of bass at the Basin at the opening of the season.

"Woody" Wilson of Speedway City, Ind., says "This is the best place in the world to rest and the fish bite ALL the time and ANY time."

"This is my favorite fishing spot and I come up here every chance I get."
Here are some of the big ones that didn't get away."
                      Ab Lessard,
                      Calumet City, Illinois

"I sure love to catch those fighting bass."
                    "Mose" Kucela
                    Osceola, Indiana

Like the thrill of landing trout? There are several springs in the lake, as well as Joe's Creek, Bohemian Creek, Slapneck Creek and Johnson Creek which empty into the lake, where you will find fighting rainbows, German brown and speckled trout.

THE HIGH ROAD TO ADVENTURE

"I have dreamed of a place almost like this, but this is even better than I dreamed of."

Frank E. Hartup
339 S. Auburn Street
Indianapolis 41, Indiana

How To Get Here:

From:

WISCONSIN Via US 41 to Jct. M 67, to Limestone

MACKINAC BRIDGE Via US 2 West to US 41,
North from Rapid River to M 67

THE SOO Via M 28 to Jct. M 94 to Jct. M 67

MARQUETTE Via US 41 South to M 67

Getting Them Ready For The Frying Pan

For information and reservations, write to:

**Paul and Grace Munier
9848 Bradbury Drive
Indianapolis 31, Indiana
Telephone: TErrace 9-0260**

Hunting Is At It's Best Around The Basin

No thrill can match the thrill you get when you see that big rack of horns step into an open glade before you—or walk up on a black bear feeding on chokeberries—the sharptail grouse or partridge breaking away from you like a feathered bullet through the trees—the honking of big Canadian geese—ducks flying over by the hundreds. Whatever your favorite hunting may be — deer, bear, partridge, grouse, ducks, geese, snowshoe rabbits, you will fulfill the moments you have dreamed about here in Michigan's finest hunting area.

If you are the kind of fisherman who would rather just sit in a boat and wait for the fish to get on your hook, there are pan fish galore —just waiting for you.

If you don't want to fish ALL the time, there are lots of things to see and places to go— Pictured Rocks at Munising — Historic Grand Island in Munising Bay—Grand Marais Sand Dunes — AuTrain swimming beach where AuTrain river empties into Lake Superior—beautiful waterfalls—Alger County has more waterfalls than any other section of Michigan.

Bring your camera and plenty of color film!

BOATS

Our boats are 14' metal Pioneer boats with air tanks. One boat is furnished with each cabin. Additional boats available by day or week. We also have Evinrude and Johnson motors for rent by day or week. Life cushions furnished at no extra cost.

CABINS

Cabins have one or two bedrooms, living room, kitchen, Philgas lights, refrigerators, 4 burner gas ranges with oven, built-in cabinets in kitchen with sink, and either gas or oil burners for heat. All linens are furnished except dishcloths and washcloths. Cabins will accomodate from 2-6 people. These are the only cabins for rent on this lake.

Cabins are open from early spring through deer season. Reduced prices during September and October!

GROCERIES AND SUPPLIES

You can buy milk, bread and some groceries at Limestone, which is 3½ miles from the cabins, or additional supplies at Trenary, about 10 miles from the cabins.

The Honeymoon

The Munier's annual visits up north were special. Dick grew up and began sharing the places and customs with his new bride, Jean. The setting: July 5th, 1959.

As young newlyweds, they meandered their way to their honeymoon destination ... Limestone, Michigan. Not much has been discussed about this week, and as their eldest child, I cringe at asking too many questions, afraid they may tell me too much.

They stayed in Cabin #5 which was the cabin closest to the lake. Dick's Indianapolis neighbor, Harry Allison, his brother and friends stayed at cabin #2 during the same week. They played a "shivoree" trick on Jean as she emerged from cabin# 5 late the afternoon after their arrival. She opened their door to the noise and chaos of rattling cans.

If the pranks of their friends were not enough, the mosquitoes were. They were nearly "eaten alive." Only a slight exaggeration. Jean was awakened in the middle of the night

22

with the room rocking. Wearing only his 28" Hanes briefs and a layer of goose bumps Dick was frantically walking across the bed armed with a flashlight in one hand and the flyswatter in the other.

Although fishing is a great sport, it's not necessarily the only thing a young bride wants to do on her honeymoon. This lack of interest in fishing is not a concept males share.

Half way through the week, Jean opted to stay behind while Dick went fishing alone. It is of importance to note that, the previous summer, Dick, Uncle Bob Dierdorf and Babe Moran

Dick's Northern Pike

had gone fishing with Bill Cummins and "Carrie", from Brazil, Indiana. They were in two boats on the opposite side of the lake from the cabins panfishing. Pine needles began to fall and the elm waved their leaves in a rustling motion as if to beacon their concern. The cumulus clouds that had shaded the fisherman off and on all day became angry and the white of the clouds began to turn gray. A storm was brewing and those in the boats knew they only had a few minutes before the rain was to come. They decided to pull up anchors and return to the cabins.

Wind had picked up speed and the water changed direction. Lightening illuminated the sky and then a second later there was a sudden clap of thunder. Ripples turned to waves. About halfway across the lake, the motor on Dick, Bob and Babe's boat quit running. Bill and Carnie tried towing the others with their anchor rope. The waves had now surpassed the white cap stage and were about three to four feet tall. The boat turned sideways and began filling with the AuTrain. To avoid sinking, all three men jumped overboard capsizing the aluminum boat, "Grace."

All tackle was lost and Dick caught the anchor rope with his foot. Grasping the overturned boat he finally managed to shake the anchor loose. Thank goodness they were within sight of the cabins. Fred Rowcliff came to their rescue and everyone survived the ordeal.

Knowing of his near drowning, Jean, "Puddin," became frightened when Dick didn't return at the time he said he would. You see, he is generally a punctual person. The first half an hour came and went, then an hour. Jean began to consider the possibility of being widowed on her honeymoon.

Finally, he came rowing home with a stringer full of fish. "I'm sorry I'm late, Honey. The fish were biting and I just couldn't stop."

Lesson # 1 - Priorities.

She was able to forgive him and that very night, along with his fried perch, sunfish, fried potatoes and onions, Jean served the most fabulous delicacy a young groom could have imagined ... a relatively new concoction called Jell-O. The flavor was orange and it contained fruit cocktail. Dick was very impressed with her culinary skills. To this day, Dad raves about this dessert. Even as I write, I find it hard to imagine my parents this sappy.

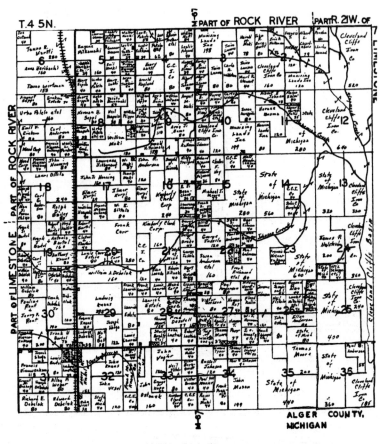

1950's Plat Map

The quaint one bedroom, red-roofed, white-washed 16' X 16' bungalow, from this week forward, would be known as "the honeymoon cabin."

Jean says, "We also found several nice little islands." I'd prefer not knowing...

In Trenary on U.S. 41 just fifteen minutes south of Limestone are six cabins known as the Snow Bird Motel. These one room efficiency cabins are self contained with a kitchenette and full bath. Their knotty pine walls remind me of Grandma's. They are nice, clean little bungalow type cabins.

The current two person rate is $33 a night, weekly rates are $180 and monthly is $300. John, my husband, and I stayed in cabin #5 this past spring. We had not called in advance, but were lucky to find a vacancy.

The owner was out on errands and had left a note on the office door to just go inside and make ourselves at home and she would catch up with us later. Are people that trustworthy now a days? The Barretts, owners, are lovely people. For reservations call Steve or Sandy at 906-446-3315. Go ahead and try them out sometime.

Cabin #5

This little cabin still holds many memories for this couple. It is a special place because of the sharing that occurred that beautiful, "chilly" July as they began their new life together.

Upon entering the cabin, the guest finds a newly recovered plaid Naugahide sofa, Formica table, four chairs, gas Frigadaire, stove and lights. The smell of sulfur permeates the air as wooden matches are struck to light the gas ceiling lamps.

The illumination casts shadows on the cedar walls. Freshly caught panfish pops grease as it fries in the blackened cast iron skillet. Fried potatoes and onions gently simmer on the second burner as coffee percolates on the third.

The bedroom consists of one full- sized bed. It has just been "made up" with crisp line dried sheets and an off white knotted Chanelle bedspread. The dreaded bedpan or "white owl," as some know it rests under the bed. Of course, the outhouse is out back if one prefers (which I do).

Cabin #5

Dozens of picture collages line the walls of the living/eating area. Some are glued down and others tacked to the corkboard base, but all pictures are yellowed by time, their corners curled. Perhaps the guest can feel a connection to the others who have come before. The sparkle in their eyes faded only by the age of the pictures. Prized catches are displayed.

The faces of only a few winter visitors shine as the winter sun is reflected from the snow. Those hardy souls who vacation here in the winter join the locals around November 15th. Their quest is for the 12-point white-tailed buck, the black bear, or the large Northern pike living beneath the foot deep ice, hungering for warm earthworms.

Fresh water is plentiful. The hand pumped well is only fifty yards away. The red paint allows it to stand out in contrast to all the green of the surroundings. The well pump is elevated three concrete blocks and a masonry table about three by five foot allows for the filling of buckets, or the washing of clothes or fish. It is centrally located to each of the cabins. The water is always crystal clear and ice cold.

Don't get me wrong; Cabin #5 isn't anything really special. Following the long secluded winter a heavy cleaning is necessary in preparation for the new season. The door is unbolted and despite the fall cleaning, one is greeted by the smell of mildew and stale cigarette smoke. Hundreds of insect corpses and an occasional mouse that was unable to escape its eventual death of cold cover the floor. It's not long before those odors are replaced with the fragrance of Pinesol and freshly line-dried linens.

For years, Ethel Birk and occasionally other ladies, helped Grandma clean the cabins. Ethel usually came once a week to clean and was paid $125 a month.

Climate and Terrain

There is not much of a spring in Limestone. It seems as though winter arrives directly from summer and escapes it just the same. One can recognize spring by the melting snow, the return of the birds and the arrival of new born sheep and calves next door. Whippoorwills call to others encouraging them to come home for spring. The green of grass is a little slower to come.

In spring and summer, mosquitoes are fierce. The comfortable temperature's ranging from the low 70's in the day to the 40's at night, are their perfect breeding ground.

In summer the temperatures are moderate. Majestic seagulls return to their summer home of abundant lakes and food source. The summer doesn't last long. Spring, summer and fall run together and make the tolerable season from about mid-May to mid-September.

Come fairly soon, the summer dies down to a rapid Indian Summer. The sumac is one of the first plants to turn red alerting the fowl that it is time to head south for the winter. Red Devil Paint Brushes sway among the deep blue Asters and deadened grasses. This time of year nearly skips fall and heads quickly into winter, getting extremely cold.

A field of wildflowers on the way to the cabins

Every closet in the U. P. contains long Johns, wool flannel shirts, heavy pants, camouflage, waders and down filled insulated jumpsuits.

The average winter temperature is 20 degrees above zero. Even though it is sunny most of the time little melting occurs. Snowfalls range from 60 to 200 inches a season. Forty degrees below zero plus temperatures allows some snow to remain until almost Memorial Day, especially along the Great Lakes.

It is not unusual for the snow to reach the rooftops. "Digging out" is an ongoing act. If let to accumulate for more than a couple hours snow will not allow the doors to budge open. It is common to receive a call from a neighbor who has been "shut in."

The land is comprised of a mixture of hardwood, primarily white birch, oaks, and maples, plus a variety of pines. The most common are the Blue Spruce, the Norway, and the White pine. A variety of fern are abundant.

The terrain is fairly flat with occasional hills and dips. A road map appears to illustrate the highways as veins in an effort to connect this place to the remainder of the body of humanity.

The night life is extremely active ... and I'm not referring to the people. Bear and deer co-exist with various fowl, moose, skunk, squirrels, raccoons, coyotes, wolf, rabbit, bobcat, mink, beaver and the wolverine. The wolverine, a fierce mammal, is Michigan's state mascot.

The northern lights are visible on clear summer nights, without the glare from any neighboring city hampering this exquisite light show. This phenomenon, aurora borealis, occurs as arches of light, from the sun, are deflected in the uppermost atmosphere in the northern hemisphere. These light patterns actually roll off the earth's protective atmosphere. It is quite a sight to see and is more visible the closer you are to the pole.

Brilliant stars hang heavy in the sky as the light fans across them much like hundreds of shooting stars lighting the otherwise dark night sky. The big dipper holds its cup full of darkness as the large full moon slowly rises overhead clearly illuminating the open fields.

The Cabins

Winter in the U.P.

One Thanksgiving, we visited Grandma. We left Indy on November 22, 1972. Mom and Dad cursed under their breaths the entire trip. The snow increased and the driving became more hazardous every inch of the way. By the time we arrived, the snow was to the roof of her house. We were thrilled. Real SNOW! The jeep was parked in the newly plowed drive. A shoveled path led to the front door.

Since the main living area of her home was raised four steps, the view from the upper living room picture window was a continuous blanket of blinding white until it reached the stand of trees entering the woods a half a mile behind her home.

We had the time of our lives. We snow shoed, rode snow mobiles and tobogganed Blue Berry Hill. But, most importantly we dug snow tunnels — big ones! We could easily crawl trough the maze and when we dug out the top we

Atop Blueberry Hill

could stand without being seen. The snow packed solid much like that of an igloo.

I'm sure either my brother, Mark, or Dad could remember who earned the title of "King of the Hill" on our snow castle. Even though I'll never forget how cold my ears were, how my muscles ached or how my toes burned with frost bite, the memories are great. Isn't that always how it is, the beauty of the past?

During winter, the primary modes of transportation are the four-wheel drive vehicle, cross country skis, snow shoes and snow mobiles. Michigan now has many designated snow mobile trails and using them is much like going skiing for vacation. For more information on these snow routes check out the Alger County Business Directory at munising@ munising. com or call information for specific phone numbers at (906) 555-1212.

The People

This is not a place for the weak. Only the strong survive the harsh, long winters and the lack of companionship. The ancestors chose to settle in a climate much like that of the "old country" they immigrated from. These people, predominately "Pals," "Swede," "Nords," and "Slovakians" explain two things: Their descendants' ability to adapt to the climate; and the unusual names listed in the local phone directory.

French explorers, and copper and iron ore miners, settled the area. "White man" also came as trappers, fur traders and loggers. The first to live in the U.P., the Chippewa, Ottawa, Iroquois, Ojibwa and Huron Indians, made this their home.

Father Marquette was responsible for making these diligent Indians Christians.

From Copyright @ 1979 Mackinac Island State Park Commission, in 1671, French Jesuit missionary priest,

Father Jacques Marquette left a small settlement at Sault Ste. Marie and established his mission at the Straits near present-day St. Ignace. He and Louis Jolliet paddled their canoes west a few years later and discovered the upper Mississippi River, a venture that assured them a place in history.

Local Indians traded their rights to the land for annuities in the Treaty of Washington...

Indian children were trained to enter the mainstream of American life...taught them not only the three r's, but practical arts as well. For the boys it was black smithing, tailoring, farming and shoemaking, while the girls mastered sewing, cooking, and other household tasks.

During the 1800's, as part of the civilization process of the American Indian, Indian agents were hired by the American Government to oversee the process.

Henry R. Schoolcraft, as Indian agent at Mackinac in the 1830's doled out the currency, medals, and necessities of life to tribal leaders, be he did much more. He studied the Indians, questioned them exhaustively about their ancestry, legends, spiritual beliefs, hunting and fishing techniques, and lent a sympathetic ear to their painful adjustment to the white man's life. Then he compiled his findings in a multi-volumed work entitled, History and Statistical Information ... of the Indian Tribes of the United States, which the new Smithsonian Institution published in 1851. It was and is today one of the best references on 18th and 19th century Indian life.

A young poet at Bowdoin named Henry Wadsworth Longfellow, fascinated with Schoolcraft's work, wrote the long narrative poem Hiawatha.

The Moral

Although the mosquitoes are worse than anywhere else I've traveled, they don't stop the pilgrims of their annual Moral mushroom hunt. This short-lived season of, perhaps, two weeks occurs each May. These delicacies are abundant, popping up in the woods by fallen Elm trees and under the umbrella of the Mayflower.

Not unlike any other sporting event, the proper uniform is donned. Hiking boots, pants, long-sleeved shirt and cap with mosquito netting. Rubber bands are used to tighten shirt sleeves and prevent pests, including ticks, from making a new home on your arm. Equipment includes *Deep Woods OFF* mosquito repellent and a shopping bag preferably with handles.

A stick is necessary for prodding amongst the damp undergrowth of mulch from fallen and decomposed leaves. The perfect mushroom prod must not be too heavy to carry or too light or it will not be strong enough to maneuver through the compost. This stick may also be used as a weapon to fend off the occasional snake startled from its slumber.

Locals laugh at the tourist paying $20 a pound for fungi. After you read a little further, I think you'll agree that it seems a fairly inexpensive price to pay. The hunt may be unnecessarily hastened by the pests, the participants over heating due to their extreme overdress, the high humidity or out of frustration.

If you haven't witnessed the hunting frenzy it is something like this ... people are scurrying about the woods, gently, but quickly poking about the ground. These sly Moral's hide. Should it be unseasonably warm like it was this past spring when John and I ventured north, or perhaps too dry, they will not appear. If one is not discovered in the matter of about 45 minutes then there probably aren't any. However, tomorrow may be a different day.

After a rain, they may poke their heads through the undergrowth and the two to six inch fungi will appear. At this point they are abundant and will grow in clusters. Time and need/greed only dictate when to stop the game. This year's score: Morals 7 - Tacketts 0.

Thank goodness Dad had saved a freezer bag full of these mushrooms just in case our trip had proved futile. The smell of the Moral lightly floured, salted and peppered frying in sizzling butter and olive oil make the wait worthwhile. It is difficult if not impossible avoiding the temptation to reach for the mushroom before it is removed from the frying pan.

Morals

Notable point: Other mushrooms habitats have been duplicated in caverns and caves, however the Moral has not.

Only as long as Mother Nature provides the environment will they exist.

For more information on this and other wild mushrooms contact Superior Wild Mushrooms, in Traunik, at (906) 446-3328.

The Quest For a Simpler Life

As Dick and Jean began raising their family of three children, they, too, began making the annual pilgrimage north. In the 1960's, before the days of the interstate, the 600-mile journey normally took twelve hours, plus.

On more than one occasion, car sickness prevailed. There was the time I was forced to use my brand new cigar box (transformed into a crayon box) as a waste can. It wouldn't have been so bad had the discarded crayons not landed in the back window of our 1964 Oldsmobile Dynamic Eighty-Eight. They were forgotten and left to melt, diminishing the resale value.

By the time the third child arrived, the Bartlows were experienced vacationers. They improved their trips by purchasing a Vista Cruiser station wagon. Four inch foam rubber served as a mattress when the back seats were folded down. The ride was made easier on the children — and maybe the parents — by leaving right after work and driving through the night. Their arrival left the children remarkably refreshed.

In years when Dick and Jean braved daylight trips, highlights included:

1. Viewing the "Sears" tower, in Chicago, Illinois.

"Kids, this is the tallest building in the world!" And, several hours further north, the Green Bay Packers Stadium. Both of these sights were appreciated from the highway. Who has time to stop?

It was a long drive in between some of these stops. I just wonder how many Bottles of Beer were on that wall? We counted hundreds. Other road games we played were Riddlede-Riddlede-Re, I see something you don't see and the color is _____. This was fun until after awhile the creative genius of my brother, Mark, led to the color of brown which no one could possible guess was on the cow he spotted a mile back. In an all-out effort to avoid World War III, Dad would offer, "Let's see how many different states we can spot on license plates." Mom chimed in, "How about Simon says?" At this point, I just preferred another nap.

2. Mars Cheese Shop, on Interstate 94, just north of the state line, in Wisconsin.

I can still remember the smell of cedar as we walked inside the gift shop. Mars is from Europe and his shop embellishes a style as well as feel of Europe. They have a restaurant, gift shop and bar. Their specialty is their cheese, wine and beer. Today, on rare occasions when I enter a Stuckey's the aroma of cedar drifts out the door and I experience deja'vu.

However, as a kid, I vividly remember, being impressed by the ability to purchase a genuine oyster in a can. I recall the sales clerk's patience as I counted my loose change to purchase my two-dollar treasure. She used a can opener and had me remove the oyster. Then, she cracked the shell with pliers and carefully pried the shells apart with a paring knife. I imagine my eyes grew wide with joy as she removed my very own, slightly misshaped pearl. I still have the pearl, which currently resides in a small box with my bicuspids.

3. Spaghetti dinner in Germantown, Wisconsin, just north of Milwaukee and a few miles off the beaten path.

In the sixties, it was a treat to "eat out." Our favorite dinner spot was this family owned Italian restaurant. Besides the wonderful meatballs, the experience was made greater by the fact that we all wore bibs ... even Dad.

4. Oconto, Wisconsin, to purchase fresh smoked Chubb.

The store where we purchased the fish, was located on the north side of the river. The owners of the store/bait shop were triplets. These brothers received their primary source of income fishing commercially. A Chubb is a white fish that is netted from the Oconto River. The average fish is about a foot long, including the head, and are smoked whole. We usually bought a half dozen.

After purchasing the smoked Chubb, we drove about a half an hour to Marinette, Wisconsin. Two large concrete Belgian horses with log sled in tow greeted us. We stopped at the park. Now that I'm a parent, I'm convinced Mom and Dad used this as an opportunity to let us expel pent up energy. They would prepare our lunch/snack, depending on what time of day it was, as we played. They removed the fish from the waxy butcher paper. Our fish was accompanied by a block of the Mars Colby cheese and Zesta crackers.

We each had to debone our own fish, except for my little sister, Pam. She could eat the tender meat as quick as Mom pulled it from the bone. And, truth be known, even at the young age of three she was probably as quick and skillful at the task as the rest of us. We learned early to be careful with the sharp, tiny bones and always have a piece of bread close by in case we got choked.

Our departure led us across the bridge into Menominee, Michigan. On our way out of the area Dad always pointed and said, "Kids, Fox River is the only river, in North America to flow north instead of south." My dad was so smart! Even at a young age I thought this a valuable piece of information. I remain hopeful that it will appear as my "Trivial Pursuit" question.

5. As we approached our destination, we left our last big city, Escanaba.

One last pit stop. For the last hour we head deeper into the woods as we follow Lake Michigan northeast. Lake Michigan is wonderful. Depending on the season, temperature and time of day, it displays a variety of personalities all its own.

6. Finally, Rapid River, Michigan cheese factory.

The odor still permeates my senses. A cheese processing plant smells like a mildewed dish rag. I recall biting into the freshly processed Colby cheese curds and wondering how something that smelled so bad could taste so good.

We turn due north, at Rapid River, for the final 30 minutes of the drive. The houses become smaller and more worn by years of hard weather. Each has an attached covered and enclosed porch about four by six feet to house coats, boots and shovels. This is also where the children wait on the schoolbus. The houses are sprinkled further and further apart. This was my favorite part of the journey.

The familiar sights brought us closer to our destination. Even though the sights remain the same coming and going, year after year, I always looked forward to them. Knowing what to expect gave me a sense of security.

John in Marinette, WI

To the right is the gray house with the Frigidaire in the front yard. This is where we buy the small red fishing worms. We turn right to go through Trenary. On the southwest corner is Herb's Tavern. We cross the main street and on the left is the Trenary State Bank and the Trenary Home Bakery. We're through town. The road makes a long sweeping 90 degree angle left so we're going north again.

To the left is the strawberry patch. Sugar maple trees are being tapped and the metal pails hang from the taps. Soon the cauldrons in the field will have fires under them as the sap is boiled into Maple Syrup. In September the same pots will be used to turn apples into apple butter. These two canned products supplement the northerner's incomes during lean winter months.

Only five more minutes. We spot the clearing on the right as seven straight blue spruce act like sentries guarding the entrance to Grandma's. I see her silhouette in the kitchen window and watch her face brighten with a smile as she hears us pull onto the gravel drive. We have finally arrived.

Life in the U.P.

The Other Cabins
Cabin #1

Cabin #1 was my least favorite cabin, of the five. Perhaps it was because it was not in proximity to the other cabins; or because of the way it sat back into the woods; or it could have been all the dead mice each week when Grandma and I cleaned. I don't know exactly why, but the place just gave me the creeps.

This "camp" was frequented by many black bears. You see, when people from the city came to rent the cabins, they didn't understand the need to bury the fish entrails, setting up oneself for disaster. Bears are unforgiving when it comes to a late night snack. No trash can is too large a challenge.

Actually, I didn't spend much time here so I can't even describe the inside, maybe I just simply don't want to remember.

One good thing came out of Cabin #1 — Mom and Dad's current oak kitchen table. When Grandma sold the cabin, she gave the pea green enameled table to them. They spent the Blizzard of 1978 stripping and refinishing this beautiful piece of furniture. I remember Mom sanding feverishly until she removed the name "Bob" that had been carved into it. This lovely round topped table makes a beautiful centerpiece in my parent's kitchen.

John and Deb in front of Grandma's

Cabin #2

Cabin #2 is a different story. As you drive down the steep gravel road from #1 and make the sharp right turn, cabin #2 is the first one you see, even before seeing the lake. Always painted green, the exterior looked like any normal 1940's house in rural America. It was constructed of Masonite pressed board shingles and once slept the greatest number of guests.

I have great memories of the time our whole family was visiting and our cousins, the Testys, met us at the cabins, the week of July 22 through July 29, 1967. They stayed in cabin #2 while we were in cabin #3. There were three of us Bartlow kids and four Testy kids. Our ages interspersed so that there was one of us every year from eight years old to one. We were in sequence Jennifer, Debbie, John, Mark, Bethany, Pam and Brent. We looked like a row of ducklings toddling behind our parents whenever we went places together.

Our mom and theirs, Cecelia, filled brown paper grocery sacks of freshly popped corn and thermoses with Kool-Aid or hot chocolate. At dusk, we all piled into the station wagon to go to the dump. If we were lucky, we might see a family of well fed, stout, brown bear.

Bear wait around and observe until all is quiet before making their appearance. As they emerge from the woods they lift their heads sometimes standing only on their rear legs as their nose sniffs out any possible threat. Generally the parents rummage for food and then motion for the young to join in their scavenge. Bear generally travel in pairs with one to two cubs in tow.

Some evenings we headed to "Old Joe's," a "family" tavern. Now it might seem odd for parents to take their children to the tavern, but that was the only other place available.

We loved it. At least there was entertainment, ranging from shuffleboard to pool; where else can a kid learn to polka? I think I'll go into this topic a little later ... it deserves an entire chapter in itself.

We played cards frequently! If you don't know how to play cards, in the northern woods you're lost. By eight years old I was pretty much an expert at euchre' and of course solitaire. The "Michiganders" played Smear, a card game similar to Euchre, and pinochle.

There was no television reception, telephones, or any other new aged device at the cabins. Even if there had been, there was no electricity that far down to the lake. This actually forced families to become closer. We had to talk and play — not much else to do.

I remember going with the Testys to Lake Superior. There is a great little beach area in Munising. Even in July the water's cold. We kids didn't mind, but the parents stayed away from the water. Mom and Cecilia tried to tan their faces yet stay covered with beach towels to keep warm.

Once my little sister, Pam, who was two at the time decided she was going into the water. When we were all occupied she just took off running straight into the depths of Lake Superior. She continued walking straight into the water until it was well over her head. Her skinny little body did not float. I can remember this in slow motion. I'll take the credit for pulling her out of the lake, although it could have been John. I like it much better being a hero instead of just an average bystander.

One of our favorite things to do at the beach was to bury ourselves in the sand so that only our heads were exposed. "Kids, be careful or your lungs will collapse." Do we all have the same parents?

I thought there were many beautiful green polished rocks. After hours of beach combing, however, I discovered they were pieces of 7-Up bottles, polished, by the sand. What a disappointment! This past May, my husband, John, and I strolled the beach collecting our own private collection of Lake Superior keepsakes. And they are beautiful in the Pier One glass jar covered in water.

When I recall cabin #2, I think of this special week. Years later, Grandma and I watched the volunteer firefighters attempt to put out the flames that engulfed Cabin #2. We held each other and cried. Without speaking, we mourned for the times and the people that were no more.

Cabin #3 and #4

Cabin #3, a red stained log cabin ties with cabin #5 as my favorite. Across the drive path from cabin #2 and right beside cabin #4. It was almost always rented as the cabin of choice. The well was right outside the front door.

I can still remember the sharply pitched squeak of the screen door and the sound of it slamming shut with each use. I liked it's floor plan the best. It was fairly large with two bedrooms and a large living area. The kitchen had a double stainless steel, stove/oven combination, refrigerator and cupboards. The floor was covered in gray and pink linoleum tiles. In the living room was a gas heater, neat little studio hide-a-bed sofa and wooden kitchen table with two bench seats.

Before the grandparents had their home completed we had the treat of staying at Cabin #3 for a week, in 1967.

Today, if I lie down by an open window and close my eyes tightly enough, I can hear the wind whipping over the lake causing leaves to rustle; feel the air tickling my face as the breeze comes into the window; and sense the filtered sunlight reaching through the trees to warm my skin, all of which takes me back a lifetime ago.

Cabins #3 and #4

Cabin #4 was almost identical to #3, but for some reason just didn't project the same personality to me. Perhaps the view was not quite as good, maybe we hadn't ever spent a night there or perhaps its proximity to the well made it just not as memorable.

However, Cabin #4 was closest to the cleaning table —a definite advantage to the avid fisherman. The table was made of hardwood. This was by far the best place to clean fish for the table area was large. A bucket was provided so rinsing the table between cleanings was made easier. A military shovel lay underneath so the burial of the waste nearby was convenient.

The Incident

The summer of 1967, our entire family went to Michigan for our vacation. I haven't mentioned the road on the way to the cabins, yet. It is important in order to describe the next episode of this story.

After you turn off the main highway, the road goes from gravel to dirt in a half mile. Now if you went straight, you'd go to the dump. If you were on your way to the lake, you'd turn left past the abandoned house where that crazy guy died, then past the field of wild flowers. The road up to this point was barely two lanes. If you were a foreigner and didn't know where the crazy guy lived, you'd take the first (and only) left. Are you with me so far?

After the turn, it was obviously one lane, a wide one lane, but still only one. Let's call it a four mile lane instead of a road, so you can have a clearer picture. After the first turn, the lane becomes fairly dense with pine and hardwood trees and undergrowth. In short it's snaky and in high traffic season, in order to be acknowledged, you need to honk before entering the turns. If the honk is acknowledged with another, each vehicle pulls as far right as possible and proceeds slowly forward.

Mom and we three kids were on our way to the lake. We must have slept in, for the sun was bright and the heat was radiating off the road. It was about noon. Dad and Grandma were already at the lake. They had left the house no later than 6:00 a.m. Remember, the adage "the early bird get's the worm?" Well, men are most certain if they're not at the lake early, someone else will get "their" fish!

49

Since it was mid-morning and Grandma had some help around the cabins, she decided to head off to town to run some errands. She forgot the all-important honk ... and, so did Mom. Let's just say Mom and Grandma's incident (well, okay it was a full blown head on collision) almost knocked us kids silly. We thought it was funny until Grandma and Mom both began crying.

Grandma's new yellow AMC Rambler was totaled and our white '64 Olds Dynamic Eighty-Eight was without a scratch. Thank goodness the speed was only 15 miles an hour. Even though the accident could have been serious, once we realized everyone was okay, everything was fine. My sister, Pammy, kept laughing. As a matter of fact, I'm certain Grandpa Paul and Dad used this story to their advantage many times.

It is October 1, 1967.

Letter to Agnus Paullus, sister, from Grace.

10/1/67

Dear Sir,

I have started several letters to you & by the time I get back to it, it would be stale. Things have settled down now so hope to finish this one.

I want to thank you for the Ozette Fall awards, the Boy scout & the Purly Anniversary card. Paul has really enjoyed the Ozziorn. I got a big saw full & he wash a little help from Luke gets loaf of it.

Sure glad to hear that Barry & Shirley have a long overawl Dixon will be a little father to Luke. Mom & Dad said they moved. What is their new address?

Why don't you get in your car & drive up here? It would be good practice for you. Come though.

Well here by my trailer window I'm sure you would enjoy sitting here by my trailer window & just looking. The trees are turning all colors & mixed. In the evening when the sun sets on the hillside across the lake & the trees are reflected in the water, it is a breathtaking sight. I think you would like our home too.

We have a big picture window overlooking

the woods. Our living room isn't completely finished but we sure had a fire in the fireplace several times. It is so pleasant to sit there, even though outside is all witty there, no dogs on the floor, no diapers. I can imagine what it will be like when it is finished & we can sit there & watch the snow flurry through the trees & maybe as dark as this wondering out. Mom said she could just see Paul & I sitting there this winter — Paul eating popcorn & me knitting & rocking in front of the fire.

We have almost decided not to go South this winter. We will come home before Christmas but we might come on back after we rest for awhile. There are so many things to do at the house for we hardly clothe anything must inside. I can't do too much work until the furnace is in & that probably won't be until the end of October as we are thinking of coming back & getting the house in by that time. It will be time to start on the cabins, so we haven't settled at all.

-3-

I mean the kids so very much. I gave him so close to them so so long makes it worse but for that we where. I hope next year they will let Debbie & Mark stay awhile. It was such a wonderful week till week Debbie was here week all. I had so much enjoyment just watching her explore everything. Did I tell you that when they got her about 4:00 in the morning she didn't want to go to bed. She wanted to just sit & talk to you. And as we did. Excellent fishing & Debbie & I watched the sun come up. Drew a wonderful aquarium though her eyes for it was the first animal she had watched.

What a different life this is compared to Indy! Although I miss everyone, the time goes so quickly. I can't believe it is Oct already. We have worked harder than we did at home & lots of it hard work but we still find it empty. We have both lost weight from swimming so much but we eat more, you should see Paul eat! At home Paul just he eat him. At home he didn't eat much he ate or not & now he is always asking when we are going to eat.

-4-

for breakfast. I always fix 8-10 strips of bacon, 4 eggs & 5 or 6 pieces of toast & then kids eat the left. Smallmouth are go out & catch a mess of fish, come in & fry them. There have been days when we wouldn't like working real hard & planned to work all day. Then we would loaf at the lake & it would be so calm & nice we would just drop everything & go fishing. What a wonderful relaxing feeling to know you can do things like that. I'll probably get so relaxed I'll get fat & lazy. People think I'm on the run, do I know. I had to either slow down to their pace or have a nervous breakdown. You are matched too for the hours, etc & you are lucky. If you've got a 30 & 4 market, in other markets the fight things done but they don't seem to worry me as much if they aren't done.

While we are away & you have time, I'll try to answer some. Next time I'm still a bit swept home in the day to do all that I want to do.

Have a happy birthday. Stay home
Jean

THURS NITE
6/27/1968

DEAR DEBBIE,
HOW'S OUR BIG GIRL DOING?
I HOPE YOU ARE ALRIGHT &
STILL CATCHING LOTS OF FISH.
WE ARE FINE DOWN HERE.
MOMMIE HAD TO WORK AGAIN
TONIGHT. SHE WORKS FOUR
DAYS THIS WEEK, BUT IS
OFF SAT & SUN. I AM STILL
WORKING 50 HRS. A WEEK.
HOW'S GRANDMA GROCIE,
GRANDMA & GRANDPA D.?
TELL THEM HI FOR ME.
HAVE YOU SEEN ANY DEER?
THERE WAS A RABBIT IN
OUR GARDEN THIS MORNING
EATING OUR GREENS I
RAN HIM OUT. I MAY HAVE
TO HAVE RABBIT STEW
BEFORE LONG.
MOMMIE, MARK & MOM
TOOK THE CAR & GOT A
NEW MUFFLER & TAIL PIPE
ON IT TODAY. WE'RE TRYING
TO GET IT FIXED UP FOR
THE TRIP TO MICHIGAN.
JUST THINK, JUST TWO
MORE WEEKS.

(2)
IT HAS BEEN COLD &
RAINY HERE TODAY. IT MUST
BE IN THE LOW 50'S.
MARK, PAM & I HAD A
PARTY TONIGHT. WE HAD
POPCORN & POP.
YOU WON'T KNOW OUR
GARDEN. IT SURE LOOKS GOOD
VIRGIL'S TOMATOES ARE
REAL PRETTY.
WE GOT A NICE LETTER
FROM LINDA & DWIGHT.
THEY ARE FEELING BETTER.
JEFF IS TALKING A LOT
NOW.
WE GOT A NEW BACK
TIRE FOR MARK'S BIKE.
IT WAS JUST WORN OUT &
THE SPOKES WERE BAD
PEPPER IS JUST FINE.
SHE IS GETTING BIG.
SHE CAUGHT A SMALL
MOLE THE OTHER NIGHT.
HOW'S TOBY? IS HE
BACK TO NORMAL NOW?

(3.)
IT SEEMS LIKE YOU'VE BEEN
GONE A YEAR. A LOT OF
PEOPLE HAVE ASKED ABOUT
YOU. KAREN SURE MISSES
YOU.
WELL SUGAR, I'M ABOUT
TO FALL ASLEEP, SO I'LL
CLOSE FOR NOW. WRITE
WHEN YOU CAN & BE
CAREFUL. "GOODNIGHT DEB"

LOVE,
DADDY

Goodnight Debbie
Love
Mommie

Letter from Dad and Mom to Debbie
June, 1968

53

My First Trip Alone

My first trip north with Grandma was one I'll never forget. It was June 5th, 1968. I remember the date because we were in Wisconsin, about half way to Limestone, from Indianapolis. It was to be my second summer vacation spent with Grandma. We were in the Jeep listening to the radio when an urgent news report interrupted the music. Robert Kennedy had been shot. He was dead.

His assassination upset Grandma. She was so distraught that she pulled over at the next rest stop. When she broke down, I felt so helpless. Grandma was a very devout Democrat and a proud American. She had already suffered the assassination of President John Kennedy, a few short years earlier, and the uncertainty of the United States' deeper involvement in the Vietnam crisis. Plus, the hippies were rebelling. This turmoil represented changes in our country and loyal Americans like Grandma became fearful and confused.

Grandma and I didn't resume our trip for about an hour. We sat in silence for several miles. I laid my head in her lap as she continued weeping, not knowing what the future held. I remember her stroking my hair as she drove. Somehow, her responsibility for me gave her comfort.

I Thought Matt Would Never Leave

Thinking of cabin #3 reminds me of one family that usually rented the cabin for a month at a time. I thought perhaps my memory was playing tricks on me so I checked this thought against Grandma's journal. They reserved the following time periods:

6/29 -7/27/68	6/28 -7/26/69	7/4 -8/1/70
6/26 -7/31/71	7/1 -7/15/72	7/21 -8/4/73
8/3 -8/17/74	6/21 -8/16/75	6/19 -7/10/76

I was so looking forward to meeting my new playmate, Matt Telliga. It is 1968. I had met his parents before. Things I already knew about him were that he was a year older than I, was very smart and had blond hair ... which Grandma said made him "very cute." What I did not know about him I learned very quickly. They arrived one bright afternoon as I was playing catch with Toby, Grandma's Brittany spaniel.

I knew almost immediately that we wouldn't get along as he exited his car, turned to me and stuck out his tongue. He sure had the grown-ups fooled. Try as I might to like him, by the end of his two week, too-long stay, dislike had turned to near hate.

This cute little, blond-haired, blue-eyed boy was one of the meanest I had ever met! He took great pride in frying grasshoppers with the reflection of the sun through a small silver-trimmed magnifying glass. He almost exuded joy at stepping on baby birds after they had fallen from their nests. And, he loved to mutilate fish and crawdads (all this, of course, before they were dead).

He was staying forever. "Nope, Grandma, I will not show him my island, my tree house or my other secret spots." This rebuttal was met with slight disappointment from Grandma as I am certain she really had hoped that I would have found a friend, for the summer, and she genuinely liked his parents. But, I stood firm and refused because I was as certain then as I am now, that he would have somehow destroyed my special places ... maybe even the whole forest.

I escaped him by traversing over fallen logs heading deeper into the Hiawatha National Forest. I would watch for the sign of moss on elm trees and be wary of the possibility of crossing the path of a rattler or black bear. No challenge was too great compared to the escape of Matt. I knew that the further I wandered as long as I turned to the left and kept walking I would end up at the lake. I could always turn back and follow the shoreline to the cabins.

There were only a couple times I was glad he was there. When it rained and all of natures creatures were safe, we'd play cards, or if an adult were present, he was actually civil.

Okay, one more time, I believe it was 1974. What! He was only staying for two weeks? Rick was helping Grandma mow and take care of the grounds and was paying attention to me—it was perfect. I must have hit puberty ... need I say more? I'm just glad he was there for only a couple weeks because I sure would have hated to have grown to like him.

The summer of 1977, Bill and Mable Wyatt rented cabin #3 from June 4th through September 3rd. By this time I had reached High School. My time was divided between home and other activities and Michigan seemed so far away. My trips became further apart and now my brother, Mark, and my sister, Pam, had taken my place. That is the last I remember of Matt.

I get melancholy thinking about how I thought he'd never leave and secretly wishing he had stayed.

Grandma's House

The white frame house was trimmed in red and black. The steep pitched roof did not have gutters. This allowed the snow to glide off instead of settling in place, the weight of which might be its demise. Facing the house, to the left and up four steps, was the original entrance into the house.

This old entry was no longer used. The original living room was to the left, but had been converted to a guest bedroom. It was filled with modern blonde furniture and elegant table lamps.

To the right was the modest kitchen. Stained redwood cabinets each with a stainless steel latch ran along the south wall that adjoined the living room. Where an exterior window once was, Grandma kept various styles and colors of vases and potted ivy. This opening added much needed light into the room.

A small table sat under the window that looked outdoors into the front yard. On the wall beside the leafed table was a wall telephone. Opposite was the stove/oven and small preparation counter top. Various canned goods were stored underneath in the cupboard. In the small hall off the kitchen and facing it was a combination office and laundry room.

Walking down the short hall one finds a small full bath with shower and the master bedroom. Each room was well appointed and on the dresser in the master bedroom was Grandma's jewelry box, beautiful perfume bottles and a mirrored tray.

Grandpa's addition to the house included a bi-level living room off which the garage set and could be entered through the lower level. The upper and lower level and the four steps separating them were divided by black rod iron. Gold looped carpet adorned the upper level and steps.

The upper level had a large plate glass picture window facing the woods out back. Forty wooded acres of timber and wilderness lay just past the fenced back yard and thicket of white birch. Just north was the neighbor's open field of grazing sheep and cows. Occasionally, deer would mingle with the domestic beasts, neither seeming to mind the company. Glorious sunrises could be witnessed through this window.

A couple gold wingback chairs, matching sofa and a green upholstered chair accompanied the two magazine end tables and coffee table. The focal point of the room was a beautiful fire place, beside which was a wood box that could be filled from the garage.

One enters the home through the lower living room. Its floor was tiled in off white with gold veined twelve inch tile squares. This area is where Grandma kept her organ, by the door to the garage. The organ was a concession for her black baby grand piano. She loved the piano, but it would not have been practical to keep, nor would it have made the 600 mile journey well.

Above the organ, on the wall, were black musical notes touting an erratic rhythm. The music stand had sheet music opened to either Englebert or Simon and Garfunkle's "Bridge Over Troubled Water" and ready to play. Classical records were in order with most frequently played on top of the record player stand. Music had always been an important part of Grandma's life.

On the opposite wall next to the steps was a short open book case/curio cabinet of sorts. It was painted an off white color to compliment the colors through the room. A mantle clock that chimed Westminster was its centerpiece.

An orange and red glass bowl rested on one shelf with a darkened piece of driftwood that appeared like a fawn lying asleep in grass. Many books about birds, flowers, trees, motivation and travel were lined vertically as well as horizontally, propping others in their respective places. Each book was signed noting Grace Munier as owner.

The travel books were marked with labeled sections, by country or topic. Key destinations were underlined. Above the cabinet were two pictures of streets in France. A place only dreamed about. The trade-off was a retirement home in the northern woods.

Under the large plate glass front window rested the glass top table. Grandpa Paul had made the glass-topped table out of a piece of a driftwood tree stump. He had found the perfect piece after months of searching about the AuTrain Basin. It is a beautiful piece of furniture, one of four Grandpa made in his lifetime. He floated the stump until it made a level water mark, and he cut away the excess tree. Then he did the other side to make it a level 18" high. It was inverted so the roots face upward.

Grandpa sanded the rough edges and painted it. The top was designed by sitting the base upside down on a refrigerator box and outlining it in marker. The glass cutter, Cook's Glass Company in Indianapolis, rounded the edges of the cut glass so it made an unusual and safe table top.

Under the glass were two separate potted philodendrons whose vines grew rampantly with the west sun filtering through the picture window. They clung to and intertwined with the arms of the driftwood.

The only time I ever remember missing home was my first summer alone with Grandma—the summer of 1968. After the first two weeks of my stay, we were headed out the door on our way to the cabins. I stopped, at the doorway, leaving the living room of her house.

Setting there on the glass-topped driftwood table, was a floral china demitasse set and a glossy painted Olin Mills picture of our little family. Pictured were Daddy, Mommy, Mark, Pam and me. I vividly remember thinking that I couldn't remember how their voices sounded. One quick call home to hear their voices, and I was cured.

Jay and Dorothy Miller, Harry and Betty Allison, Mom and Dad, and I own the tables. I am often reminded of my strong family ties and reminisce when I look at my table, one of the most treasured heirlooms I possess.

Grandma had a stroke in June of 1982. She was not yet 65 and had no health insurance. Slowly each of the cabins were sold off, the 40 acres at Cabin #1 and the two parcels of land by the house. Dad and Grandma kept the land her home rests on and the house until all of their combined assets were depleted. Only those who have been forced into this awful reality know how hard it is to let go of their home.

In 1988 Tim and Danita bought the house. The pine trees out front are no longer short enough to jump over. They tower over the numerous gardens like Babe the Ox guarding Paul Bunyan. Tim and Danita have transformed the garage into a shop and operate The Limestone Herb Company. Their gracious spirit and presence are reminiscent of another couple deeply in love and enjoying life to its fullest.

My hope is that they will perpetuate their love of the place and the feeling of family and friendship that can overcome boundary lines and distance. Their gift shop and nursery has something for everyone from plants, dried flowers and herbs, teas, oils and gift items. Please support them by calling (906) 439-5448. Or, next time Limestone is on your way, take the time to stop and say, "Hi, Deborah sent me."

The Trailer

An 8' x 36' silver aluminum trailer with pink trim became our daytime home. The unfurnished bedroom held all our fishing gear along with extra rental equipment. There was no water hookup so extra life vests lay in the bathtub. The toilet re-mained closed and a water pan, filled daily, rested in the sink. We heated the well water in a tea kettle on the gas stove. Since there was no electricity on the road to the cabins we used gas lights, stove and refrigerator. The end of the trailer had a sofa that extended the length. It could fold out flat into a narrow bed.

Grandma Gracie getting ready to go to the trailer

There used to be a large tree right outside the front of the trailer. Each morning Grandpa would plug his electric razor into the tree and he would sing while he shaved. Little did I know, eh? I'm not sure if he did this to trick the kids or if he wanted to get a reaction from his guests. Well, it made sense to me because phone poles were made out of trees I thought electricity just ran through them. Remember, I was just seven years old.

Just to the other side of the walkway of the tree was a charcoal grill and picnic table that beseeched anyone around to come and sit a spell. This place always attracted others and was used to rest or just visit a spell.

Grandma and I had a ritual before leaving the house each morning. This included gathering our clothes for the day, a cumbersome task. Our daily attire included a variety of shirts, shorts and pants, boots, shoes, bathing suits and jackets. Our shirts were of various lengths and weights due to the unpredictable climate. We always threw in extra socks and underwear in case an overnight stay at the lake became necessary.

The final provisions were a loaf of freshly baked cinnamon bread, coffee, milk, luncheon meats, enough extras for supper, and any other staples that were running low, at the trailer.

Then we filled up the white Jeep pick-up with gasoline from the big tank in Grandma's back yard. The Jeep was Grandma's trademark. It had a bass painted on its doors and advertised the Au Train Basin cabins.

I watched the most incredible sunrises from the kitchen window as Grandma and I had our coffee and cinnamon toast. We used this quiet time to read our mail that we had picked up on the way to the lake. Most mornings we wrote letters to family and friends. Sometimes we read, but mostly we just shared the peace.

The lake would be so calm this time of day that it looked like a piece of glass. The reflection of the trees mirrored themselves against the perfectly still water and if you looked at it long enough you could not tell here reality started or fantasy began. The colors were even more brilliant than the sunsets.

Navigating the Au Train

The diversity of the lake made fishing and boats of all types common. Canoes glided across the open expanse of the waters and through tree stumps turned into driftwood. My grandparents owned and rented to others 14 and 16 foot riveted aluminum boats. They used 10-20 horse power, Johnson and Evinrude motors. Only when the lake was extremely high did water skiers try to conquer the lake. Many large, fast bass boats navigated the AuTrain.

Grandpa's secret trout hole was on the side of the lake opposite the cabins. The first time we went there was the summer before he died. He had purchased an old pontoon boat

Jean, Pam, Debbie, Mark, Dick and Toby

and made repairs to the old drums and pieces of steel. He used his metal-working talents that he had honed at Link Belt.

The pontoon had a steering wheel. He let each of his three grandchildren wear a skipper hat and take turns steering. When we were not wearing the hat, he was captain of the mighty vessel. He navigated through fallen tree stumps and was prepared for almost any peril.

We learned nautical terms, including bow, starboard, leeward and stern. We were careful to use proper boat etiquette and walk carefully on board. Captain Paul demanded safety.

Our destination was the trout hole. To get there, we crossed to the lake's other side where the boy scouts used to camp, and then we turned left. We stopped before we saw the decrepit old tree where the endangered bald eagle nests. We knew we were over the top of one of the coldest and deepest spots in the lake for the water gradually turned a deep shade of blue. For novices, this is where rainbow trout like to hang out.

I searched for this spot many times after this day but never did

relocate it. Grandma knew where it was but kept it her and Grandpa's little secret. This was where she'd go fishing alone. When she returned from these solitary trips, she would be somehow more at peace. This was Grandpa's lake. He owned it with his heart and soul. As it was a part of him and Grandma, it became me, too.

The Smells at Grandma's

Now I can't exactly differentiate the sequence of my visits or the years they occurred. We went to Michigan once a year for vacation before Grandma and Grandpa moved there. They moved there in 1967 and I visited often. Grandpa passed away the following spring.

After Grandma was widowed, I was sent to Michigan for the summer to "help" her and keep her company. I can't imagine how much help they thought a skinny little eight year old would be. But, I'd like to think that I was her saving "Grace." I felt so important and special when I was with Grandma.

In the solace of that wonderful world full of giving people and with nature and life happening all around me, I never forgot or really missed the comforts of my home and family. I realized in a different kind of way that I had an extended family and that, no matter what, we were still connected.

My most vivid memories are conjured by my olfactory sense — cinnamon, for instance, takes me back into Grandma's kitchen. She and I baked bread two times a week. We mixed the ingredients, then placed the mixing bowl into the sink of warm water, covering the bowl with a cheese cloth to hasten the first rise.

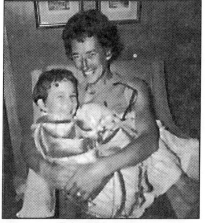

Deb and Grandma

Then, we took turns kneading the bread. The previous procedure was repeated. After the bread rose again, the fun began. We rolled the bread with the rolling pin, sprinkled the cinnamon and sugar, and placed the dough in the loaf pans — two large ones and a small one for Debbie. Told you I was special.

I debate only whether the cinnamon bread smelled best while it was baking or when we took it to the trailer each morning and toasted it in the toaster oven as Grandma's coffee percolated.

Here's another one for ya: The smell of split oak in the fireplace, just started with lighter fluid, and accented by the smell of a wet dog. This reminds me of giving Toby a bath and then having to take another one myself. It's summer, but there's a chill outside. There's a fire in the fireplace and Grandma and I have just settled down for the night.

We've halved a cantaloupe and the center of each is filled with vanilla ice cream. Our daily milk and potassium ritual. Now, I'm not sure if that was a Northern thing or a Grandma thing. As far as I know, she might have invented it when she was pregnant with my dad. I do know that next to peppermint stick ice cream, it's my favorite, too. The electric blanket is set on 10 and by the time I've finished, the bed will be ready and so will I. I haven't slept that well since.

My Friend, Rachel Bennett, and her Poetry

Mrs. Bennett was my very best human friend next to Grandma Gracie. She and her husband Bill met Grandpa and Grandma years earlier as they shared their Michigan vacations. She was a tall slender lady with short gray hair. Although her structure was large she was a very gentle woman with a soft spoken manner and spirit.

After Grandpa died, she, and her large gray Great Dane, Gus, came to visit Grandma once each summer. Betty Allison and her white, toy poodle Misty were also there during the same time. Toby, Grandma's white and tan spotted Brittany spaniel, played for hours with his friends.

After Toby's friends left, he pouted and was into more mischief than ever before. One day he came home yelping with a nose full of porcupine quills. His nose had not yet healed from the plier adventure than he returned with the stench of skunk. It was terrible. We filled a wash tub with tomato juice and bathed him until he was tolerable.

Lucky and Me; Misty and Betty; Gus and Mrs. Bennett

When Mrs. Bennett wasn't visiting with Grandma, she spent time with me. We shared a common love — rocks. Big rocks, small rocks, shiny or dull, smooth or rough, we loved them all. I used to love to find pretty rocks underwater, but was often disappointed when they dried and were dull. Mrs. Bennett showed me that if I kept them

Deb and Mrs. Bennett

in a glass bowl with water they would remain pretty.

The Christmas after she showed me this little trick I asked Santa to bring me a rock polisher. From then on I was hooked. That thing used to tumble and roll making the most awful racket until I was forced to move it into the garage.

Grandma called Mrs. Bennett "Squeek." Although her real name was Rachel, I felt it proper to call her Mrs. Bennett. She was so full of grace and eloquence.

Another passion she aroused in me was poetry.

Over the years, I have tried in vain to locate her. In an effort to preserve her wonderfully passionate works, I have printed them exactly as she wrote them; I know she would approve. I pray that the sharing of Mrs. Bennett's words may comfort others as they did Grandma Gracie. Her poetry is located following my text, in the appendix.

The Summer of the Turtle

Nature, life, birth, death and rebirth were daily occurrences that somehow I never took for granted. A new experience of growing and feeling of one with the world helped me mature.

There was the summer the large turtle came walking out of the lake. The turtle walked several yards before climbing up to the top of "the mound." It was created when the inlet was made to ground the boats. The mound was also a resting place for the anchors that were thrown out of the aluminum boats.

A single tree grew from the middle of the mound and beside the tree sat a wooden box housing life vests. This mound was about three feet tall with an oblong thirty foot diameter. A cairn of limestone, Geods and other basic rocks six to ten inches round lined the sides.

I thought this turtle very dumb. It staggered and climbed what must have been a ten story turtle's building up over the jagged rocks and crystal Geods until it reached the sandy, soft dirt. I thought this climb would have exhausted it. I would have tried to help him had I known for sure where he was going or what he was doing. Besides, Grandma had warned me of a turtle's bite. Exhausted as I'm sure he was, he started digging a hole.

I was in disbelief so I ran to the trailer to get Grandma. I thought this was good news. Upon our return she informed me that this was no ordinary turtle. He was a she and she was pregnant. Sure enough, this foot long turtle began laying eggs. This was a gigantic turtle compared to the ones I had owned. The others had been purchased at the Danner's 5 & Dime and usually lasted until their shells became soft and I was greeted with a floating turtle in a glass bowl upon my return from school.

She was either too tired to care about us humans watching her or she realized that we were harmless and only curious, for she didn't stop. She was on a quest. The eggs squeezed out one at a time and honestly looked like rubber as they wiggled out and plopped into her freshly dug hole. I gave up counting after forty.

Upon completion of this task, she used her back feet to cover her eggs with the sandy dirt then very slowly ambled down the hill and back into the lake. Grandma explained that she would not return to check on her young. I cried in disbelief and took it upon myself to be the guardian of her eggs. I made sure to check on them first thing each morning to be sure they had not fallen prey to evil forces.

Alas, one morning I was devastated to find the hole disturbed and "our" egg membranes everywhere. Again, dragging Grandma from her peace, she came to the rescue. Our babies had hatched and made it to the safety of their new home in the Au Train Basin lake.

Grandma was right about one thing. The mother didn't return to check on her eggs; but the summers I returned to my second home in the woods, I witnessed her annual ritual of laying eggs in the very same spot.

The Brisson's
Vic and Emma

Vic and Emma lived across the street from my grandparents. Their family had been in the area for years. Vic's parents, Joseph and Mary Brisson, as well as Vic and Emma have their final resting place at the local cemetery. The town of Limestone was predominately comprised of their descendants. Their house is where they remained the rest of their lives.

This milky colored two story frame home sat just off the highway. The overgrown shrubs made it impossible to enter the front door. Besides family always entered through the back, off the kitchen. The house was old, but warm and I believe Vic grew up in it. It smelled a combination of mustiness, moth balls and fresh baked bread.

As far back as I remember, they were older, grandparent figures. They were so very different from my very active grandmother, a young fifty-five years old. Vic and Emma were both short; Grandma and I were skinny and tall. I loved visiting because our heights allowed them to envelope me in their hugs. I liked hugs, so I tried to visit them daily.

Vic would tell me stories of killing big bear and Emma would just smile and say, "Ya, Ya, Vic." People talk funny in Michigan. I think it's humorous, especially now that I live in Arkansas, that they used to have trouble understanding my "southern accent." Well, my Indiana dialect is a far cry from a southern accent, compared to those from Arkansas.

Emma always had something baking and food was always on the stove. I loved how the Brissons would giggle and cuddle one another. This was no ordinary house. It was a home filled with lots of love. The house actually bowed on the sides because there was so much love inside.

I think Emma prized herself in taking care of Grandma and acting as her surrogate mother. And, of course, who can resist the love of two grandmothers every day?

On a recent return to Limestone, I was pleased to find Billy Boy, their grandson, living in Vic and Emma's house. The tall red barn is still the same. The family used the building to dry deer and bear. The house is now covered in a light taupe/gray vinyl. The once overgrown yard is manicured and even has an area fenced. They would be so proud. And, yes, almost their entire family still makes Limestone home.

Mary and Barbie

Buz Brisson was Vic and Emma's son. Buz and Edith had a daughter, Mary, who was two years older than I. Mary had many siblings, mostly teenage boys. I can't really remember how many children there were because it was as if every teenager around congregated at their home. But, I do remember Jim. He mowed grass for Grandma sometimes. It made an impression on me to have such a large family, especially one with so many boys in it.

One time Grandma must have thought I needed some companionship my own age. She dropped me off at Lillian and Harold Antilla's house, the location of the Limestone Post Office. I was to spend the day with their daughter, Janice, and Mary. However, Janice was not home, so Grandma let me walk a quarter of a mile to Mary's house.

When I arrived, Mary and I were hungry so she fixed us a hamburger in a skillet. Wow! My parents never would have allowed me to cook on the stove, let alone on a gas stove. She and I didn't have much in common, but I liked her just the same. I liken us to the city mouse and country mouse. Looking back I feel almost sorry for her as I'm sure she felt obligated to spend the day with me.

After we finished eating our hamburger, we walked to the cabins. The walk is about a five miles from Mary's house down the dirt road. It wasn't long until her uncle, Billy, brought his daughter, Barbie (she was a year older than I), to join us for the rest of the day. We did have fun.

Mary's cousin, Barbie, was a daredevil! She loved a dare. I thought I'd literally die when Mary dared her to dive off the dock into about eight feet of rough water. Fully clothed, wringing wet, leeches and all she came out giggling.

I think Barbie took after her daddy, Billy. He had a fire engine red Camaro. I rode with him only once because by the time we had arrived at Chatham I was just thankful to be alive for he flew like there was no tomorrow. He drove his sports car in the local parades. It was quite a prize. I'll not forget the parade route circling town twice and Barbie and Billy Boy sitting there doing their best parade wave.

Jan 16 Warmer 10 above 5PM. Mary and Leroy here. 15 below last night. Agnes has flue, Dick called, Grace fell and broke her wrist 2 places

Jan 17 Warmed up today 8:30pm 45/0. Cloudy all day. Went to store. Agnes here this am

Jan 18 Warmer today up in 40s. Bob Patsy and Susie here this eve

Jan 21 Went to Graces gone 3 weeks

Feb 13 Mary Leroy Anita Bob Patsy Susie here. 30/0 today cloudy

Feb 14 38/0 am. Warmed up to 54 today

Feb 15 Rained some in night. Colder 17/0 6PM

Feb 16 warmed up today 40/s 30/0 10pm Agnes here

Feb 17 54 today rain 6pm 40/0 Hartlop here

Feb 18 high 37/0 snowing 63/0 35/0 got card from Grace. Susie birthday 10 years old

Feb 19 2 inches snow. Cold 32 high 28 in pm

Feb 20 Dick and Bob here for dinner. Nice day, played cards. Mary and Leroy here. Cary gois to SC 150 mile from mother

Feb 21 Got new rider mower today 50/0 today. Colder tonight.

Feb 22 nice sun shining. day hig 31 low 30

Feb 23 slick this am. Melted 35 now 9pm. Went to town. Agnes here last eve

Feb 24 nice cool day above freezing. Susie has chicken pox. Sourwine theatre burned Feb 23, 1967 showing My Darling Clementine

Feb 25 Cloudy rain this PM. Warmer. Dallas Jane Anita and Mark here. Sure had a good game of smear, I won

Feb 26 beautiful day. Snowed last night but all gone today. Mary here 40/0 today 28/0 last night

Feb 27 Low 18 high 50. nice day. Susie has chicken pox. Went out for dinner

75

Limestone

Located in the middle of northern Michigan, Limestone, population 23, offered little entertainment. What was important was family. This family was not related by blood but connected by choice.

People just don't impose on their neighbors or drop in unannounced. But, they do share. Grandma was often greeted home with a venison roast or a sack of potatoes, sitting on her doorstep. The "Wolverines" are generally very private people. However, if someone is in need, they're ready to help.

In Limestone there are no hotels, no grocery stores, no restaurants or movie theaters, no bowling alleys or shopping malls. There is the Limestone Baptist Church which could accommodate thirty or so if needed. It is only attended on Sunday or when there is a need to marry or bury. The Limestone Cemetery, across Highway 44 is the final resting place of many of the fine souls mentioned within these pages.

Limestone's metropolis consists of four major buildings. They included the church; Dot and Murt's gas station, complete with general store; the post office and Old Joe's.

To help pay her bills in the winter, Grandma ran Dot and Murt's store for a couple years. On January 16, 1971 she fell while shoveling snow and broke her wrist. By reading her father's diary I know that several surgeries followed. I can see the healing process in her writing as it progresses and the switch to left hand by observing her journal entries.

Now called the Limestone Mini Mall, the store is pretty much the same. The facade has been improved, but the contents haven't changed. The store contains canned goods, jerky, fishing tackle and we even purchased our fishing license at the store.

Limestone Mini-mall

Now this country store beacons to the wayfaring stranger with an illuminated Mountain Dew sign. Bud Light and Pepsi signs are joined by the ice machine. On the other side of the entrance is a pay phone. A bear skin is nailed to the split cedar exterior and a couple of lonely gas pumps are positioned in the drive.

The post office, across the north side of the Highway, is inside the Antilla's, where the post office boxes are on their glass-enclosed front porch. Progress has even entered the upper peninsula. Since the Antilla's have retired and the 911 emergency broadcast system entered the community, the post man now delivers mail. The 49816 zip code resides in Chatham and 49891 mail is delivered from Trenary.

Old Joe's

Then, there is Old Joe's. As far as I can tell, an institution in itself. Buz's claim to fame was Old Joe's. He owned the tavern, which was about a mile north of Grandma's. On a map, it would appear halfway between Trenary and Chatham on Highway 67. This is what might be thought of as the watering hole. As the Cheer's theme song says, it was a place "... where everybody knows your name ..." To me, the people there were family. There was always the feeling of being welcomed.

The building itself was a simple frame rectangular structure colored like a red velvet cake. The vertical neon light beckoned people to come within. The large oak door squeaked on its large rusty hinges and ever so slowly opened. Cigarette smoke drifted out the opened door. Those seated on the cracked red vinyl bar stools would direct their attention as the squeak announced the entrant.

The quiet was soon replaced with the continuance of local gossip, jokes and visiting. The new arrival was always greeted with the tip of a hat or a hug. The spirit of these people was not dampened by the lack of employment or by near poverty. They knew they would somehow make it through the tough times just as their ancestors had before them.

Opposite the bar was a shuffleboard game half the length of the room. The floor was covered in gray tile squares. The ample remaining room was great for dancing. We locals could slide easily to the polka, Johnny Cash or George Jones. The singers' voices resonated from the juke box and echoed off the walls. This room could have just as easily been the family room of someone's home. People came for many reasons. We came to socialize.

Behind this room was a corridor that housed the unisex bathroom. It was never dirty. The corridor led to another large room, a mirror image of the bar. Its only occupants were there to play serious pool. This room was large enough for two pool tables and gave the players ample elbow room to prevent brawls.

Pug and Norm Roy were regulars at Old Joe's. Their full time home was in Escanaba, but they kept a modern "camp" on the road to the cabins. I can't think of Old Joe's without smiling about them.

Norm was a jolly little man, much like Vic Brisson, except that Vic no longer drank much. It was a rare occasion when Vic consumed a "shorty" Miller. Pug and Norm liked their drink. Pug would get a little loud and very lovable when she drank. I didn't always feel like being her dance partner, but since Norm wouldn't oblige her, I often felt it my duty.

In a highly pitched, fast paced, nasal tone I can still hear, "How 'bout that Jim, Mr. Olsen sued Mrs. Olsen for divorce. The judge asked him, 'On what grounds?' and he said, 'Her coffee is awful!'" The jokes were so bad that their lack of humor brought everyone to their knees.

"Hey Norm, Did ye' here the one 'bout the old guy that married the young girl? Well, she left 'im. She said he was dangerous as he carried a deadly weapon."

"Louie, a wife sued her husband for stealing her brassiere and selling it. Well I ain't sure what she did 'bout it, but now she's got no support."

Then there's Junior Johnson, the logger, who was as big as a "grizzly" and cuddly as a stuffed bear. He always reminded me of Paul Bunyan because he was a wonderful mixture of burly and shy, and could give the best bear hugs. Somehow this combination man/child just seemed bigger than life to me. I find this combination fitting to his character.

Junior lived in a mobile home across from Pug and Norm's and just before Howard Parr's place. His home was next to Tom Roy's deck encased A-frame. Even as I aged, I confused him with Jerome Johnson.

Anyway, so next Junior said, "The tie said to the hat, "Oh, go ahead, I'll hang on." He was booed.

"That reminds me," said Jerome, "Two little pigs went to a party, but they left because it was boaring."

And the bantering went on and on until they started repeating the stories they had told the day before. "Oh, Jees Herb, just have another one and sit down."

Tinny would just sit at the bar and visit with me while the others played. He was a great big shy guy who used to give me sticks of chewing gum. I guess I loved him best. He was so quiet and I somehow felt he understood me better than most other people. I can't even remember anything special that we talked about, except that he seemed interested in me. He enjoyed my stories and used to ask questions about my family, Indiana and my life there.

I think like many others from these parts, he had never traveled outside of this region. I guess he lived vicariously through me. Our family vacations had taken us places he had only heard about.

Pug has since passed away, but Norm still resides in the same house. The road to the cabins is now called 26th Road, thanks to 911. The tavern has burned twice since. The old timers I knew and loved have been replaced with young. It will never be the same and this is one of my greatest disappointments.

Beer

Grandma didn't keep hard liquor at the house. Perhaps she limited herself by having to pay for drinks at the tavern. She generally drank gin and tonic at a price of 25 cents a glass. My coke cost ten cents. Gosh, for a dollar we had a night on the town.

Grandpa had been an avid wine and beer maker. In Indiana, in the spring, the fields are full of dandelions. I would get paid a quarter a grocery sack for the powdery yellow tops. The greens we cooked like spinach or collards, with a little bacon grease, salt and pepper. The tops were used for making wine.

One night I was awakened in their home by the sound of a burglar, crashing through the garage throwing things. Grandpa, in his red pajamas ran through the house until he got out of the way of the culprit. Beer bottles were exploding everywhere. That batch must have had too much yeast.

He passed his refined beer making skills to Grandma and me. She supplemented her bar drinking with homemade beer. I don't want anyone to think she was a "lush" because she wasn't. Social drinking was a part of the local culture.

I liked helping Grandma make beer. This process occurred under her house in the storm cellar. Too many explosions had created messes in the garage. The constant 50 degree temperature under the house was ideal. The narrow red door to the cellar is on the outside of the house. After opening, it is several steps down to the earthen floor. An odor of dry dirt attacks the nostrils and dust drifts through the air like smoke until it settles. We turn on the lights and take our places so that we, as a team, act like an assembly line.

After the yeast had allowed the beer to ferment, it was time to bottle. This was the fun part. She used a funnel much like the one we used to put gasoline in the truck. I was responsible for adding one level teaspoon of salt to each bottle. This was a very important part of the process! I took my time to be sure I accomplished my job perfectly lest I negatively affect the end product.

Grandma then carefully capped each bottle with an instrument the looked like pliers except that it crimped the cap tightly onto the bottle. The bottles had to set for a few weeks before the beer was ready to consume. When she drank one, she closed her eyes; I imagine she shared the flavor and the experience with Grandpa. Although I have not acquired a taste for beer, on hot days when I mow I will sometimes have a beer to quench my thirst. The smell, more than the flavor rekindles these memories.

Chores at the Lake

I had several things that I enjoyed doing to help Grandma. One of my favorites was the worms. "What?" you might ask. Naturally, with a fishing resort you must be prepared for everything. Now even if Grandma did rent the cabins primarily to her friends, the resort was still a business and she depended on its income.

Besides boat rentals and the sale of gasoline, one of our money makers was worms. We took the boat motors for service at Terry's Riverside Resort, in AuTrain. This is also where we bought night crawlers. It seems that most people did not want to stop fishing if they ran out of bait. They preferred not hunting under rocks or driving half an hour or more to buy additional bait, especially when the fish were biting.

I guess Grandma was quite an entrepreneur for she realized we had a captive market. Before Grandpa passed away he and Leslie Birk built a three-section worm bed located out back of the trailer.

Grandma and I made bi-weekly trips to Munising. We bought small red worms for trout fishing and big fat night crawlers for pan fishing. Since we purchased these from a wholesaler, we could make a nice profit of about 15 cents per dozen. It was my job to tend to the worms.

I loved this. The worm bed was a pine bin with a door that opened from the top. This bin was in the woods. The task of worm tending was hastened by my unsuccessful efforts to outrun the mosquitoes. They swarmed me when I wasn't quick enough. The worm beds were filled with peat moss and mulch.

Each morning after coffee, I'd contribute the grounds as a dietary supplement. My worms were also fond of potato skins. On cool days, when I lifted the bin, steam rose and the fresh smell of properly worked over dirt hit my nostrils.

Besides these two perks, I enjoyed watching the wives of the customers. The husbands placed their worm order with Grandma and paid for them. I ran out back to pull them out of their nice warm beds and transfer them into the cardboard cups. I always presented them to the ladies. They squirmed — the worms and the wives. This little act delighted the husbands and caused everyone to giggle. I was an instant friend of the husbands ... one for the tomboy!

I also volunteered to bail boats. This generally had to be done upon the arrival back to the basin from a daily rental and always after a rain. I used a one pound, slightly rusty, Folger's coffee can. The grownups really liked seeing a kid work as hard as I did, and they usually gave me a ten cent tip.

At an early age, I realized that another potential for a tip was fish cleaning. I enjoyed this and was pretty good at it. Give me any kind of fish and I will either fillet it or just prepare it for frying. However, I'm not fond of cleaning catfish. Once I was horned before I ever got the hook removed. This explains the necessity for a Billy club in every boat.

The most exciting part about fish cleaning is the ability to dissect the creature and determine his last meal. What a fish consumes is very interesting. It is almost like hitting a lottery when eggs are found in a nice fat yellow perch. Most people don't eat the orange sack of eggs, so I saved them for Grandma and she would fry them with our catch.

To see if I still had the touch, I recently took the liberty of cleaning some fish when our friends were down for vacation.

Using Grandma's skinner (now at least 35 years old) I can still accomplish the task in just a couple minutes. Must be like riding a bike.

My Mud Puppy

One summer I rode north with my great Grandma and Grandpa Dierdorf. They are Grandma Gracie's parents. They enjoyed fishing off the small dock outside of cabin #5. This dock was off to the side of the boat ramp. As best as I remember, it was probably 30 feet long against the shore and 10 feet wide. Grandpa Dierdorf anchored three tree stumps to the floor and fastened green enameled John Deere tractor seats to it. This made the perfect spot for those who preferred to fish from the land.

When the water was up, it was probably a good eight feet deep, just deep enough to keep me, a non-swimmer, from getting too close to the edge.

One drizzling day we were fishing. (I always became excited when I caught a fish — something about conquering a creature and the satisfaction of a carnal need so deep I don't fully understand.) On this day, however, I became disappointed when I thought I had caught another darn catfish. They are so stubborn to take off the hook. But, when I finally pulled it up, it was one of the strangest things any of us had ever seen. Someone ran to the Jeep, sped into town to the nearest phone and contacted the Department of Fish and Game. The gentleman arrived at the cabins within a couple hours.

In the meantime, I had taken my catch off the hook and placed him in a cardboard box. He did resemble a catfish with respect to his skin. But he didn't have horns and he did have six feet! He was so cute. I talked to him and pet him praying that he wouldn't die or that they wouldn't kill him.

This was a first for our warden, too. What I had on my hands was a prehistoric, amphibious creature, in short, a mud puppy. Much to my relief he recommended we let the little guy go back home. I wish I'd had my Brownie camera.

Learning to Swim

I had always been afraid of the water. Grandma said that she had, too. But with the help of YWCA she learned to swim. The first summer I was there she thought it would be a good idea for me to learn, too. It made sense because we were on and around water constantly.

I put on my yellow and pink bikini and faded navy blue docker tennis shoes and we strolled to the sandy inlet by the dock for Swimming 101. The water was cold and it took several minutes just to get in as deep as my knees. Although it was in July, the water was frigid and our teeth were chattering. She explained the importance of learning to swim in case I ever tipped my boat. Okay, she was right, but gosh couldn't we find a pool somewhere, anywhere to try this in?

Our lesson was about as bad as I thought it could get. (To this day, I can't figure why anyone would intentionally put their face in the water.) Grandma decided she'd just better give up and resign herself to the fact that I would forever be prisoner to a dreaded bright orange life vest.

But, things did get worse as I emerged from the lake covered with leeches. I'll hand it to Grandma though for she didn't

But, things did get worse as I emerged from the lake covered with leeches. I'll hand it to Grandma though for she didn't visibly panic. We trotted to the trailer in search of the wooden matches and alcohol. Within 20 minutes, she had killed them all. That was the last of my swimming lessons in the Au Train Basin.

Charlie the Snake

Grandpa Dierdorf was handy. I'm so glad he was at the cabins the summer of '69, because this is the year Charlie found me. Howard Parr helped Grandma mow occasionally. He was kind of a general "fix it man." One sunny day he ran over a cute little light green garter snake. He yelled, "Oh, Jees!" I came to the rescue. Howard wasn't afraid of anything ... except snakes. Charlie was about to become minced meat.

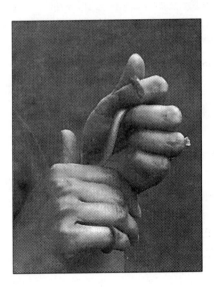

I gathered him up, all twelve inches, less six inches of tail. He didn't bleed much, but I don't think he was very happy about having to regenerate part of himself. We took a liking to each other and before long we were buddies. Grandpa's talents came in handy, because though the grandmas weren't afraid of snakes, they didn't like the idea of sleeping in the house with one, especially a curious one that might get loose.

Grandpa built a screen cage. The top fastened tightly with a wooden peg. In one end a margarine tub fit perfectly to serve the fresh water supply. The other end was covered with sand and a daily addition of fresh grass. I became pretty good at catching live flies and providing other foods that I assumed Charlie might like. It worked. Charlie grew, even his tail.

We'd play. I let him slither around my arm several times a day. As much as he liked my warmth, I liked the soft, coolness of his skin. He took three walks each day. When I was busy, the grandparents took turns snakesitting. They didn't mind much at all.

We had only one "falling out." I found a very tiny snake and added it to the cage for his company. He ate the little guy. I sobbed as I took Charlie out of his cage and was going to step on him until I realized he was probably just hungry. I added worms to his diet.

And They Came

The summer of 1969 was more than a year after Grandpa's death. An appropriate amount of time had passed for Grandma to mourn. Then the inevitable happened. The men started calling on Grandma, very slowly at first. They came one at a time and subtly.

Howard Parr, the "fix it man;" her neighbor, John Bergquist and finally Louie Johnson. These are just the one's I know about. But, one thing the men did not realize was that Grandma

was not in the market for a husband. She was very self suffi-
cient. I'm sure the thought of a companion did cross her mind.
I laugh inside recalling their coy efforts and the courting that
followed.

Howard Parr

Howard was the "handy man." I'm not sure of whether he
was being sneaky or if he was just shy. He was a sixty year old
bachelor. He would drop by the lake to help with things. He'd
tinker with mowers that I knew ran just fine or he'd mow grass
that I had just done a couple days earlier. Sometimes he'd just
inspect boats and motors just to be sure they were in running
condition, of course. At first, I thought he probably needed the
extra money. Then it became obvious: he quit charging for
repairs. Bless his heart, he was head over heels crazy about
Grandma. I loved Howard, too, but he was simply not
Grandma's type.

Then the word got out. Somehow his daily visits had turned
from repairs to "courtship," via the rumor mill. Wow! It was
like a stampede from that day forward.

Grandma was the only eligible lady for about a hundred
miles; and she owned a fishing resort. What a dream for many
men: an eligible woman and a great fishing spot! The boats
with motors were like icing on the cake.

John Bergquist

John loved pretty rocks and he began bestowing these on
Grandma and me. I guess John knew a little more about how to
treat a woman because he'd been married before. He knew how
to get on her good side. He brought us fresh rainbow trout to
grill. Now, John was on the right track. He tried to get to

89

Grandma through me, but it was still too soon after Grandpa's death for a relationship to appeal to her.

Once he brought us two big, beautiful rainbow trout to the lake. They were already cleaned. That alone should have given his intentions away. With only butter, salt and pepper in the cavity we cooked them in aluminum foil on the grill. They were wonderful.

It's funny now remembering that John left the pan in which he delivered the fish. Grandma felt obligated to return it to him on our way home that evening. She left me in the car as she walked up to the door. When she returned, her face was crimson. She had walked up to the screen door and knocked just as John turned around at the kitchen sink wearing only his birthday suit. Was his display an intentional act? I'm not sure, but he didn't show his face for awhile.

Grandma let all the men that came to court down very lightly. I really admired her for she was able to maintain very good friendships with these men for the rest of their lives. Although she was flattered by their gestures, she simply was not interested in a relationship. That is, until Louie came to town.

Louie Johnson

Louie had retired from down south, somewhere in Wisconsin, I believe. After his divorce and retirement he returned home to Limestone to care for his aging mother. He and his mother, Vangie, shared a small frame house that was next door to Dot and Murt's gas station.

Well, he must have impressed Grandma because before I knew it we were doing things with him frequently. In reflection Louie was a lot like Grandpa Paul had been. He had a similar build, was also retired, and was fairly soft spoken. He gave Grandma plenty of space, which she needed. But, he was available to take us girls out on Friday nights. I enjoyed having him around and so did Grandma. It surely was nice seeing her smile again.

Over the next few years, Louie became my surrogate grandfather. We went to Blueberry Hill to pick small pails of blueberries for pies. This was also the hill where we would go tobogganing. This must have been a very special place for Grandma and Louie because every time he'd mention going, Grandma giggled.

I had yet to go trout fishing. Besides lake trout, area lakes and streams provide brook, brown and rainbow trout. Louie's family had owned some land with a river running through it. The purling river flowed, picking up speed, until it merged into the basin. When he was a kid, Louie fished here. He and Grandma decided they would take me fly fishing in "Johnson Creek."

I swear I tried, but remember me, the mosquito magnet? We waded the creek and tried to fish, but the pests were so bad! I was slapping and scratching. I think they were both afraid I'd snag them. Finally, Louie said, "Those bugs don't like the water much." I don't think he thought I'd do it, but I plunked right down in the middle of the brisk flowing, frigid waters. They laughed until I thought they'd burst. That was the end of my creek fishing days.

Afterwards, Grandma readied us a picnic spot. As we shared our picnic, I dried there on Blueberry Hill in the bright after-

91

noon sun, smelling the fragrant aroma of sweet fruit and dandelions. The honey bees gathered their harvest buzzing from top to top not seeming to notice our presence.

Grandma and Louie kept separate households and were never married. However, they were life mates. I cherish the thought of the love they shared and their commitment towards each other. Louie took care of Grandma after she had her stroke in 1982. His family intertwined with mine. They remained together until his death, a few years later. And so it is that I also remember him as my grandfather.

Louie's Family

Vangie Bresaue was Louie's mother. She had the prettiest head of snow white hair you can imagine. She was a little hard of hearing, so when she couldn't understand what I said, she'd just smile really big and giggle. I know it had to be her hearing and not my "Southern" accent. She was so good to Grandma. Between Emma, across the road, and Vangie, they almost filled the void of being away from her own mother, my Grandma Dierdorf.

I remember Grandma and Grandpa Dierdorf coming for a visit. They must have been about the same age as Vangie. Grandpa was born in 1890 and Grandma in 1895. Vangie was born about the same time. Grandma Gracie was rolling the two girls' hair and then they decided to put up Grandpa's hair. Who says there's not much to do in Limestone?

More of my extended family included Jerome Johnson, Louie's son. He was a logger, too. Well, I guess perhaps he was a jack of all trades and maybe even the finest junk dealer from these parts. You know the type? He was so kind and playful. Gosh, I've great memories of these two men. Has life become so complicated that we can't become a little Junior or Jerome every now and then? On my last visit to the U.P., in May of 1998, John and I stopped at Vangie's house where Jerome now lives. He hasn't changed a bit.

Ray and Jeanette Radovich, Louie's daughter, lived in Milwaukee, Wisconsin, but also had a little house in Limestone for their weekend retreat. And, Grandma loved them all as her own.

My First Airplane Ride

I was on my way back home to Indiana. My return was the summer Grandma and Grandpa Dierdorf had taken me to Michigan. By all accounts, that makes me nine years old.

Well, remember Charlie? By this time, we'd been friends a good two months. I wasn't willing to let him go. Grandma decided we could sneak him on board the airplane if we put his cage in the bottom of a handled shopping bag. I then laid my orange windbreaker on top of his cage. Our attempt to take him aboard was prior to airport security.

We boarded in Escanaba, Michigan without a hitch. The tricky part came when we changed planes, in Milwaukee, Wisconsin. We had a few minutes between flights so I took him to the restroom and gave him a drink. I was sure that since the ride made my stomach queasy it probably had his, too.

Just as I lifted him from his cage, a lady emerged from a stall. She let out a scream. I was in fear that I would have to relinquish my friend — my only living reminder of Michigan. If I had been forced to give him up, I may not make it through

93

the year to next summer. I pleaded with her not to say anything and assured her that Charlie could not escape his cage. Grandma, Charlie and I made it back to Indianapolis without any more incidents.

The Storm

The summer of 1969, Rick Miller from Plainfield, Indiana, came to the cabins to help Grandma. I had just turned nine years old. Rick was so cute. His hair was a little too long. He was tall and thin, and sixteen, but I still fell in love with him. He stayed at the lake in the trailer. During the day he helped with mowing and heavy chores. He repaired the boat engines and aluminum boats.

He brought records with him during his stay. He loaned me his new Iron Butterfly record. I did not know what "IN-A-GADDA- DA- VIDA" meant, but I felt so grown up that he lent it to me. I know now that it means *In the Garden of Eden*. I wonder if he thought about the connection?

One evening Grandma and Louie went fishing and we stayed behind. They were to be back at dark, but before five the skies darkened and it began a dangerous storm. Rick decided that they were probably in trouble and did what I thought was very brave thing (upon reflection, it was the worse he could have done).

He made me wear a youth life vest over top of my rain gear. Then he loaded spot lights, flares, blankets and rope into the boat. He made me get down into the very front of the boat to weigh it down and to protect me. Then Rick covered me with life vests as we went to the far end of the lake in search of them.

We stopped after a half hour of fighting the waves for fear that we'd run out of gas. We searched in vain. He anchored us to a stump and fired off three flares. After the waves calmed a little, he steered us back to the cabins where we built a large bonfire. We had hoped this would help them and others toward a safe return.

They did return safely after waiting out the storm. Not wanting to waste the beautiful bonfire, we used it to warm ourselves and roast hot dogs and s'mores. The Brisson's walked down from their camp on the lake and joined us. This was family in the true sense of the word.

Nature's Playground

My favorite dock was off the back of Cabin# 5. Its width was only three feet, but it is was about fifteen feet long with a six foot width that made it "T" shaped at the end.

Usually after lunch and a hard morning of play and adventure, I was beckoned by the lake. Much like Huck Finn, I would grab a cane pole and half a dozen red worms and position

A Tomboy at Heart
Debbie in 1971

myself at the end of the dock in anticipation of catching a meal of "pan" fish. Pan fish might include perch, sunfish, bluegill or even a catfish.

However, the late day sun joined my full stomach and exhaustion. Before I knew it my white deck shoes were off and the 10 pound test line was wrapped around my big toe. I lay down for a nap. Most days I did not catch supper, but a few times I was awakened by a tug on the end of the line. This always surprised Grandma when I took her our "catch-of-the-day."

Right between the two docks and outside Cabin #5's window was my reed house. Here grew hundreds of reeds. My first visits to Michigan I established this house, complete with kitchen, bedroom and living room. As I aged, I looked back upon this place with humor as I reminisced at the imagination of a child.

Another of my inventions was Debbie Island—my kingdom. This little piece of heaven was up the lake several hundred yards from the cabins. It was my own secret. The journey there was very treacherous—over washed up stumps, through water, fighting off fatigue and the real possibility of an encounter with evil.

Prior to my journey to the island, I could spot intruders to the kingdom by surveying the land from about a 40 foot climb up the maple tree just outside of Cabin #5. The tree was quite tall and straight. It grew with a triple bole which enhanced my already efficient art of tree climbing. This had its advantages, for at the top, the two main trunks had joined together with one horizontal branch and provided me a perfect stoop ... the watch tower.

Dragons, bear and snakes lurked behind trees and brush. My safe haven was nestled 15 feet or so off shore and was approachable only by jumping onto stones protruding out of the depths of the Au Train Basin.

The best part of the kingdom was solitude and freedom. An occasional hawk or gaggle of Canadian geese would announce their flyby. Many birds are migratory in these parts, but many make the marshes and wetlands their year round home. Small pencil eraser-sized toads were plentiful. The seagulls and toads were my friends. They did not have a say in the daily operations of the kingdom but were good company as they listened to stories hour upon end.

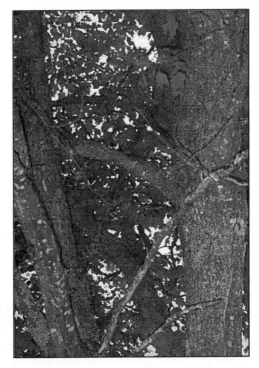

The majestic pine reaches desperately into the heavens to catch a glimpse of the sun while the sun futilely attempts to warm the earth. As ground and sun collide dust and pollen merge to create light beams and enhance the regal artistry of the spider. Once just a sapling, the tree tried earnestly to survive its fallen home of compacted soil and rock. It thrives on the once trodden path left only a relative short time ago, by the lone logger. His task was to scratch a meager living from amongst the forest floor for he was the rightful heir of his forefathers and his God.

The roads leading into the depths of the forest are almost recovered by undergrowth as nature reclaims the land. Yet, if looking close enough one sees the glimpse of two parallel lines of slightly indented earth tracing the logger's path. The only other sign of a prior traveler is a constructed fence of rocks, an occasional transplanted perennial or the remaining stump of the fallen tree. This recognition ignited jealousy at the thought of sharing the tranquility and comfort of a known route and yet a peace, perhaps one of comfort with the knowledge that a way out exists.

Usually exhausted by my journey and my thoughts, I would prepare for my return trip to the cabins. I would cross back inland and find a nice soft spot of tall "deer grass" to nap upon. (I doubt if "deer grass" is a proper name for the soft 6"-8" high grass that Grandma insisted Bambi slept on.) I learned quickly that I could take many routes back to the cabins with the lake as my compass.

The wilderness walks home usually found me refreshed and more than a little famished. I'd return to the trailer finding Grandma had completed her cleaning of the cabins before I had completed my play. A bologna and American cheese sandwich on white bread with Miracle Whip was usually accompanied with Grandma's trademark bread and butter pickles and Kool--Aid. I was now refreshed and ready for an afternoon of fishing.

While bailing boats one day, I had found a medium sized silver spoon. After the usual chores, I thought I'd try my luck at casting. On this particular day, I stood on my favorite stump while I practiced casting. My stump was located at the end of the cove where we anchored the boats. It was a huge old stump entwined with inch thick wire that had washed ashore. When the lake waters were high, I'd have to jump to it to keep from getting wet.

I was nine years old. Boy, was I surprised when, with my third cast, it hit. The fish took my lure with the power of a freight train. My adrenaline kicked in! I was so shocked I set the triple hook fast and in one swift motion jumped from my stump and began reeling as fast as my skinny little arms could reel. Imagine an eighty pound tomboy landing a 19" fish, without the help of a net. I swear it was that big.

Prior to this experience, I had only used a cane pole or my rod and Zebco reel equipped with 10 pound test line and red and white bobber to still fish. Not on any fishing program since have I seen such a beautiful sight as that 19" Northern as it gave up its fight and swam up to me. Even the Baracuda I caught in Cancun doesn't compare.

I still remember screaming and running, with fish in tow, to Grandma. The Pike had barely made the 18" minimum catch. Grandma told me that if it hadn't, we'd just have to step on the fish. She assured me that would make it grow an additional half inch to "keeper size." It's always better to be safe when it comes to being caught by the game warden. Maybe that's why we cleaned the fish immediately. Even though it was pretty bony, it sure tasted good. Grilled Northern Pike smothered with butter and wrapped in aluminum foil ... boy, it just really doesn't get any better than that!

The lake went through a period of phenomenal growth when it was not uncommon to catch three-foot Northern Pike. Other inhabitants include catfish, walleye, large and small-mouth bass, trout, yellow perch, sunfish and bluegill. Fishing at the Au

Train Basin was almost always good. And I hear some really big ones got away ... As a matter-of-fact, I know this guy that says he caught a bass so big that the picture weighs four pounds.

About a fourth of the summer mornings were filled with rain. On those lazy days, Grandma and I stayed in the trailer listening to the sound of rain pelt the metallic roof. I can vividly recall the aroma of cinnamon bread baking and fresh perked coffee as the percolator tumbled and roared on top of the gas stove.

These days were usually spent with Grandma doing book work while I wrote to family and friends back home. I also filled the day with Solitaire. After the rain, the lake calmed and was glassy. The sun peeked out and the robins began tugging at their brunch. Worms fought to keep their lives. Another day had begun. I wondered what others might be doing as we watched the world come to life. Were these images like those God witnessed as he looked down upon the earth after creation?

Chatham

Chatham Co-op was close, only seven miles up the road. Grandma also traded with the Red Owl and the Co-op in Trenary. Since everyone was family (in a community sense) she spread her business around. When she did her banking in Chatham, she'd go across the street and pick up the few items she needed to get us through the week.

The Fourth of July came to Chatham. Was I excited! The parade hailed the beginning of the festivities. There were no floats. A couple cars, the school kids and a log truck were the parade highlights. The bright red newly polished fire engine signaled the end only after completing the one block circle twice.

This "real" carnival was complete with rides, greasy corn dogs on sticks, a pony ride, mice in a maze, dart throws and games where we could use our skills to toss dimes and win real china or toss ping pong balls for a live gold fish.

Gosh, this was great fun. Grandma even gave me five whole dollars to "invest" in the prizes. I won a beautiful rose-lined saucer for her and a gold fish for me. Grandma served pickled beets on her lovely "china" saucer. The fish died two days later.

The Food Up North

I'd like two pasties! How exactly do you pronounce it? I still get confused. These meat, potato, carrot, onion and rutabaga pies are terrific. The best are made by an older lady in Chatham Corner. I have yet to duplicate the flavor, but get closer with each try. Here's a recipe that was given to me:

U.P. Pasties

The story as duplicated from the recipe goes: "Juanita (Taft) Mills was raised in Osier by her family. They homesteaded the land in the early 1900's working as loggers. The women did all of the cooking to supply the loggers and railroad workers with meals. Pasties were made because they were easy for the men to carry with them to the job site.

The ingredients were nutritious as well as easily accessible (right out of the garden!). Ground venison was often substituted for ground beef."

Pasty Crust

9 cups flour	3 cups lard or shortening
3 teaspoons salt	3 slightly beaten eggs
1 cup of cold water	3 Tablespoons of Vinegar

Cut lard into the flour with pastry knife until the consistency of peas. Add the remaining ingredients and blend with pastry knife. When I'm lazy, I just use Ritz pie crust.

Pasty Filling

6 large potatoes	1 large rutabaga
6 onions peeled	3 carrots
2 pounds raw hamburger	

Cut all vegetables in 1/4 inch cubes. Mix in hamburger, salt and pepper to taste. Roll crust in 10" circles. Fill individual crust circles with ½ to 3/4 cup of the filling. Roll crust over to make half moon and pinch edges. Bake on cookie sheet 350 degrees for 1 hour.

I like to add a patty of butter per pasty for added moisture. Other variations may include adding celery or celery salt, or the addition of cream of mushroom or cream of mushroom soup. This makes a more moist pasty.

The terrain and weather don't lend themselves to farming. With the exception of huge strawberries in June, most foods are purchased except for vegetables that can grow in a short three months or are roots. For example, carrots, radishes, potatoes, turnips and rutabaga are plentiful.

The primary source of food is from nature itself. The meat is predominantly venison, bear, fish and don't forget to throw in the good old domestic chicken. A lot of locals raise cows, too. I remember the tender venison stew or Swiss steak with carrots and tomato sauce.

In retrospect, I recall Grandma could not successfully cut a chicken, so another favorite was a whole baked chicken. With the invention of Shake 'n Bake, we loved baked pork chops. Grandma's favorite vegetable was English peas with pearl onions. Any meal went well with boiled parsley potatoes. But, one thing to remember was if these foods are not on your diet and the IGA doesn't have what you'd like you're pretty much out of luck.

Trenary

Trenary Tavern is much like any tavern or "bar" in the world. Dick and Minnie were the proprietors. I've traveled all over and have found commonalities. They exist in all corners of the world from Germany to Mexico and, yes, Trenary, Michigan. Taverns are usually a little too smoky, fairly dark, serve some form of snacks to complement the drinks, and have local music emitting from a band, a radio or jukebox.

The Trenary Tavern does have the best French fries. And, don't forget the people. The patrons are lovable, many trying to escape life while others try to live it. If no action is here you can just stumble right out the door and into the Silver Dollar.

John and I love to find family run pubs in our travels and have met some of the nicest people in the world.

Herb's brother, Francis Finlan, owned the only "real" grocery store around, The Red Owl. Francis carried the round rye bread fresh from the bakery . Wolverine Boots lined the shelves. Francis employed a butcher named Waddle. Waddle used to give me a hunk of bologna or a frankfurter every now and then.

The Trenary Farmer Co-op Store, had about everything you'd need. More than a grocery, the store carried everything from household items to food, fishing licenses, huntin' boots, fishing gear, seeds, clothes and pretty much any other household and school item necessary.

The floors were dirty, but it was almost impossible to keep them clean, taking into account the customers' muddy shoes. It was dusty in the summertime. Flies and dust accumulated through the ever opening and closing of doors. This mercantile/grocery store did not lack friendliness or local gossip. If you hadn't heard a story at the lake or had not been to Ole' Joes yet, you could find out the real truth at the Co-op.

The store had to stock a lot of merchandise because the nearest *big* town was a good 45 minutes away. This was a profitable business.

Herb's Hotel was owned by Herb Finlan. Herb was the man that sold the cabins to Grandma and Grandpa. The hotel had a restaurant on the first floor. Friday was all you can eat "Smelt" night. Smelt are small fish that are deep fried and eaten whole.

TRENARY HOME BAKERY, INC.
E 2914 HWY. M-67, P.O. BOX 300, TRENARY, MI 49891-0300
906-446-3330   1-800-TOAST-01   FAX 906-446-3361

Price List Effective 5/1/1998

Unit	Description	Price	Quantity	Total
10 oz.	Cinnamon Toast	$ 2.40	_____	$_____
7 oz.	Sugar Toast	$ 1.90	_____	$_____
7 oz.	Plain Toast	$ 1.70	_____	$_____
24 oz.	Old Country Rye	$ 2.40	_____	$_____
16 oz.	Sour Rye Bread	$ 1.95	_____	$_____
14 oz.	Italian Bread	$ 1.70	_____	$_____

Introducing ....Webber Farms Pure Maple Syrup

Unit	Type	Price	Quantity	Total
1/2 gallon	Plastic	$16.25	_____	$_____
Quart	Plastic	$ 9.95	_____	$_____
Pint	Plastic	$ 5.50	_____	$_____
1/2 Pint	Plastic	$ 4.00	_____	$_____
3.4 oz.	Plastic	$ 3.00	_____	$_____
16.9 oz.	Log Cabin Tin	$ 7.50	_____	$_____
8.45 oz.	Log Cabin Tin	$ 5.25	_____	$_____
		Subtotal	_____	$_____
		Shipping & Handling See Chart Below	_____	$_____
		Total	_____	$_____

Shipping & Handling

If Subtotal is:	You Pay:
Up to $10.00	$ 6.50
$10.01 - $ 20.00	$ 7.00
$20.01 - $ 30.00	$ 7.75
$30.01 - $ 40.00	$ 7.00
$40.01 - $ 50.00	$ 7.75
$50.01 - $ 60.00	$ 7.00
$60.01 - $ 75.00	$ 7.75
$75.01 - $100.00	$ 7.00

For Every $100.00 Please Pay
$13.00 For Shipping & Handling

Please check one:

- Check or Money
  Order Enclosed ____

- Please Bill Me ____

Please allow 2-3 weeks
for delivery. Thank
you for your order!

Please Print Clearly or Type

Ship To: Name: _____

Address: _____

City, State, Zip Code: _____

Phone Number: _____

Bill To (If different from above):

Name: _____

Address: _____

City, State, Zip Code: _____

Phone Number: _____

The bones are so soft they just go down with the rest of the fish. You can chase the fish with a little bread and butter if you're afraid you'll choke on the bones.

After supper a Polka band played upstairs. The band usually included an accordion, harmonica, banjo, bass guitar, piano and a couple of singers. Frankie Yankovic played here, too. He was cubed the "King of Polka Music." He even produced a couple record albums. Of course, the more people that joined in on the singing, the merrier. If the band were not available, the jukebox was satisfactory. Boy this place did "rock!"

There is a little bakery in Trenary, The Trenary Home Bakery, that has fresh bread daily, except on Sundays. They have even expanded their operation and have opened "Plus," their restaurant. This wonderful cafe' serves breakfast and lunch.

Their bakery specialty is a round loaf of bread. After it has been baked, it is sliced and sprinkled with cinnamon and sugar. The slices are then placed face up on large baking sheets. They again go in the oven for a few minutes to dry and harden. The hard toast this process produces is wonderful. The toast reminds me of Italian Biscotti, only much larger.

I am amazed that it is still in operation and I can even Fax my order of Trenary Cinnamon Toast. Here is a copy of their order form. Just photocopy it or give 'em a call.

Traunik

Just east of Limestone is the community of Traunik at the corner of H-01 and H-44. A historic site plaque in town denotes the Mikulich General Store. It reads:

> Traunik was the heart of a large ethnic community that developed in the early 1900s, when Slovenians who cut timber settled on the cut-over land. This store, built 1922-23, was purchased by Louis Mikulich in 1925. Mikulich's store was the social and economic center for the community. In 1927 Mikulich became postmaster and opened an office in the store. His family's residence was on the second floor. The Mikulich General Store was listed in the National Register of Historic Places in 1993.

The store brochure tells the Morgan story as: Dee Morgan cherished the warm memories of shopping with her grandpa at the old-fashioned General Store. Those fond experiences were the basis for establishing Morgan's Country Store & Museum in the Historic Mikulich Building of the 1920's.

It served a 50-mile radius of early lumbering camps selling everything from button hooks to horse bridles. Today it sells old-fashioned candies, oil lamps and parts, soaps, candles, baskets, rag dolls, cookbooks, pottery and glassware, gourmet coffees and teas, and Stulb paints just to name some of the olde tyme goodies.

The current store is reminiscent of old-fashioned General Stores that feature goods and wares of the 1890's and 1900's. From the moment you step into the quaint old building, you discover an honest-to-goodness Country Store from grandpa's days.

The selection of merchandise, unique displays, fixtures and authentic storekeeper attire make the Morgan's County Store & Museum an exciting trip into the past. Call (906) 446-3737.

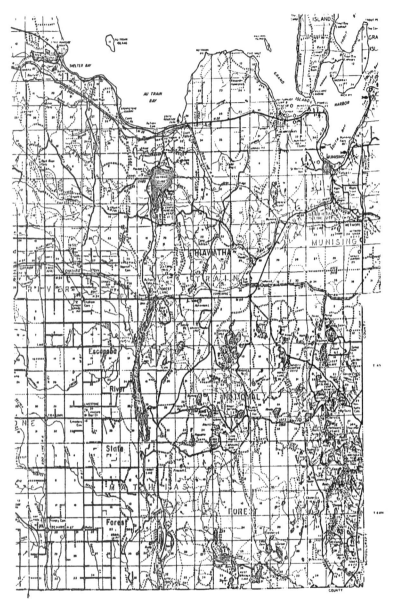

Local area map illustrating Eban, Trenary, Limestone, Traunik, Chatham, and Munising

Munising

The U.P. is bordered by Lake Michigan, Huron and Superior. Fishing in the Great Lakes includes salmon, lake trout and brown trout. The U.P. is only connected to the state of Wisconsin and thanks to the five mile suspension bridge, from Ste. Ignace to Mackinac City it is also connected to lower Michigan. Canada is across Lake Superior to the north. The Soo Locks near Saulte Ste. Marie allow passage of ships and barges through the great lakes to the Atlantic Ocean.

Miner's Castle

Munising, Michigan, is the Wood Pulp and Iron Ore Capital of the World. I'm fairly sure of this. Despite over 40 lighthouses all along Michigan's U.P. coast, for over 200 years ships have fallen victim to the Limestone cliffs. Remember the song about the Edmund Fitzgerald? This famous ship crashed into the Limestone shores just off the coast, in Lake Superior, in the year 1975.

This city also boasts the "Pictured Rock Cruise" which meanders around the Lake Superior coastline and its breathtaking glacial views. Large 200 foot sandstone and limestone walls and rock formations like Miner's Castle or cascading waterfalls like Wagner or the 250 foot Munising Falls, plus the scenic overviews provide an end to the photographer's dream.

Sandy beaches make Munising a rock hunters dream. Michigan's Upper Peninsula, Four Season Travel Planner notes, the beaches of Lake Superior are covered with agates. Banded agates, jasper, quartz and copper are among many types of rock found in the eastern U.P. Ishpeming has the country's largest outcropping of jasper. For more Michigan travel information, a current phone number is (800) 562-7134.

Wagner Falls - on the way to Munising

Alhough all this fanfare is fairly impressive, it's not what I like most about the big city of Munising. I liked best the Holiday gas station. This was an ultra modern station complete with a mini-mart. It might not sound like much, but this was way ahead of its time and a far cry better than the "filling stations" I was accustomed to in Indianapolis.

1968

1968

	Date	#	Explanation	Adv.	Fuel Oil	Burn Oil	Gas (Oblige)	Ins	Ins		Sundry Exp	Maint Roads + Trails	Other	Misc	Glat	Supp	Gas Oil	Total Exp	Insurance Stores	Cabin Camping	Family Oil	
1	Jan 22	167	Callyn Kahenes Dec. SP 70.59; RE #7345							1				11402	207			11452				
2	Mar 11		Scott							2	677							677				
3	23	207	Neil Margate Material for crucita	5000						3								5000				
4	Apr 16		Brewery Bagg Paint for #2 cabin							4			828					828				
5	18	219	Rudolph Stor act orplan	2125						5								2125				
6	17		Brewery Carl Repairs							6			388					388				
7			Brainard Stahl Roofing Cement + paint							7			257					257				
8	23	211	Bargs Bros Serv Gass							8				1200				1280				
9	27		Richmond Oil Co Gastard Order							9			388					388				
10	May 6		Woolworths							10			181					181				
11	8		Lot 4 Mante Gas + oil for motor							11							250	250				
12	12	#226	Benny Burnorts Motor repair							12		907						907				
13	14		Rudph Mount Gass for crucita							13							185	185				
14	20		Phil Mourns Cabin top							14			736					736				
15	13		Bargas Bros Pillow slips							15	241							241				
16	16		Bruan May	7125						16	920	927	2278	12600	707		435	24787	14000	3000	300	
17	17		Bruan							17									14000	3000	300	
18	18		mowing							18												
19	Jun 8		Jeni Bruan							19			1200					1200				
20			Petty cash							20	381		3200	900		252		1023				
21	21		SP State Office Boat gas + N tax							21								900				
22	12	316	L Dollins Son 1 card matches	2278						22								2278				
23	12	318	Richmond Oil Co 50 gal gas / fuel oil		3124					23							1564	4688				
24			Bruan – Gross	2278	3124						381		1720	900		232	1564					
25										25			10710					10319	9100	6050		
26	Jun 20	240	Blackstore Stripe 350 gal 1 gender Sewed 707.18				6314			26			12450					17224	9100	6050		
27										27								27448				

1

Even better than all this was the free, official, regulation baseball given with each self-service fill-up! Wow! I didn't have to do a thing except fill up the Jeep with gasoline, regular, not ethel. This is trickier than it sounds. Grandma bought all of her gasoline wholesale from the Gladstone Skelgas man. He always gave her a fair price and she filled up her own holding tank, in the back yard, once every month.

Regular gas station prices were quite a bit more expensive, especially in the city, $.24 a gallon. She could tell that I really wanted that new "official, regulation" baseball. So she scratched through her billfold and produced enough money for the fill up. This was truly a good day. See now why Munising was so special? And, Grandma, too!

Christmas

There is a large gift store in Christmas, Michigan, Santa's Gift Shop. As a matter of fact, besides Mrs. Klaus Christmas Mall and Santa's Post Office that's really about all that's in Christmas. But, there are a few things special about this place.

* Both shops carry all sorts of neat gift boxes made of cedar, Indian dolls and beautiful plastic deer that look real, Lake Superior agates and iron ore in addition to post cards.

* You can mail your letters from the Post Office and have them canceled at "Christmas, Michigan."

* It is the home of Amy, the Black Bear (who was thought to be a female), but turned out to be a male! He used to drink all the bottled pop you could afford to buy him. He's quite an attraction for he love's the water and spends much of his time

John in Christmas

cooling off in his private tub. To keep him company in the heart of Christmas is Santa's reindeer.

Grandma always stopped for me when we had a chance to drive through Christmas. The bear is still there but he's so old he no longer drinks the pop, and appears in a constant hibernation state. When we last saw him he was lying on the cool concrete floor sound asleep with one foot dangling in a tire swing. We observed him for awhile to be sure he was still breathing. Most black bears live a few short years in the wild. When we saw him last, in May of 1998, he was 29 years old.

* The local American Indians have recently opened a casino just west of town. On Ladies Night they pay $10 to each woman that comes in to register. The brown and tan facade of the simple rectangular structure resembles a storage facility. They serve free Coke and beer. Wine coolers must be purchased.

In addition to the many slot machines there are three Black Jack tables if there are enough participants available. This is a far cry from Las Vegas, but it generates a lot of income to the local economy and provides another source of employment and entertainment.

Reflection

Today, I sit here and write at my desk in Arkadelphia, Arkansas. The comparisons and contrasts are almost undiscernible. This is a remote place, too, complete with its limitations and abundances. I guess upon reflection, we all know a Limestone, U.S.A.

Thinking about Michigan is like remembering a relationship with a long lost friend — a kinship full of secrets, intimate feelings and thoughts harder to express than to take the time to recall. Grandma passed away on June 10th, 1990; a piece of me died, too.

The need to preserve this part of my life is stronger than the need to keep the passage private. How many others really have the chance to experience such oneness to a place, to relive pieces of time? A place that changes a person forever. Limestone was this important place to me; it was my "Walton Pond." It is a part of the person that I've become.

During these times I was impressionable. Events, people and places probably had the most impact on the formulation of my being. And, I had total awareness and connection with the environment and life.

My daughter, Adrienne, was eleven months old when she first set foot in the Au Train Basin. Although I doubt if she ever desires going there again, this place has indirectly formed her life as it has mine.

In today's complexities of life, I struggle with the balance of Pavlov's Hierarchy of Needs and possessing the completeness of achieving and fulfilling all my needs, with less. I am reminded of the great author, Robert Frost. I'm certain he achieved the awareness as is presented in "The Road Not Taken."

As long as the participants in this diary survive, the memories will continue to exist. Perhaps with this document, they'll be suspended in time. I hope with this printing, that I've helped in some small way to preserve our memories.

THE END

Appendix

Mrs. Rachel B. Bennett's Poetry

FAITH OR LOSS

A dark day comes to one and all
When happiness falls beneath a pall.
The soul must seek the Master's creed;
No other source can meet this need.
The sun's bright rays are cold and stark
When sorrow demands and the day turns
    dark.
The human heart can fill with dread
When a loved one's life hangs on a
    thread.
The anxious minutes are hours long.
And fear can weaken even the strong.
Faith holds the answer to all the quests
And only God knows what is best.
The darkness softens and fears allay
When we come to the end of that
    troubled day.

YESTERDAY, TODAY AND TOMORROW
(1968)

Life's day dreams fade away —
In the hours of Yesterday.
The only time is here and now
Before Today becomes Yesterday.
Wasted time brings regret,
Things undone we can't forget.
Always make the most of Tomorrow,
Before it becomes Yesterday's sorrow.
The shifting winds will change Tomorrow
And Today will be Yesterday.

DREAMING

Self relaxed and eyes straight staring,
Things undone but still not caring
Seeing not and too not knowing
What is here or what is going
Moving not yet traveling fast
In the pleasures of the past
Or we are planning things to come
Which we know cannot be done
Present and future far away
While in the distant past we stray
Work and duty are forgot
And nothing is done what is not
That is dreaming.

A HAPPY DAY
(1969)

When the day is bright
And the stars are right,
It is good to be alive.
When all is well
Where the soul does dwell,
The heart is happy as a song.
There are times like these
When the psyche is pleased,
And the day is never long.
At the end of the day
When it is time to pray
Thank God for the night 'er long.

ILL —?
(1969)

When illness appears we are most fearful;
The nights are dark, the days not
        cheerful.
These are times when we count the cost;
The pain appears and health is lost.
The future is beyond a human's scope;
We now must turn to the Star of Hope.
Our life is placed in helping hands,
In the one above who understands.
We realize that we must read
A slower pace in the days ahead.
The loss of health has far reaches;
One of the lessons that life teaches.

TODAY'S PRAYER
(1969)

Dear God, hear this my prayer today;
This is what my soul would say:
Give me courage to meet the strife,
Cares and worries that are part of life.
Give me faith not to despair
When days and nights are long with care.
Give me the might to hope
And look beyond a human's scope.
Grant that I may take heed
And gain solace from thy creed.
Place on us thy healing hands;
Help us thy will to understand.
My doubtful heart with peace instill
With thy love, teachings and thy will.
                        Amen.

SERENADE TO SPRING
(April, 1970)

My heart rejoices this beautiful day;
At last Spring is on its way!
Above is the clear blue of the sky
And sailboat clouds -riding high.
The red birds sing from the tops of trees
To the daffodils nodding in the breeze.
Tulips add their colors rare
And on the trees—the buds are there.
A soft warm breeze fans the air—
The scent of lilac must be there.
Winter is over—there's promise of
    spring
These lovely days make my heart sing.

TRUE LOVE
Dedicated to my beloved husband.
(August, 1976)

Beginning with the fresh young love of
    youth
To the ultimate end of years of truth.
Don't withhold that tender touch
To the one you love it means so much.
Strife and struggle add to the grit,
To strengthen life together bit by bit.
The wisdom of the loving heart
Senses a need though distance apart.
A fleeting thought shared by a glance
Reveals a love gained not by chance.
A tender caress from a loving heart —
What an inner joy it does impart.
Understanding thru channels of love
Is like a gift from heaven above.

OUTER SPACE
(1969)

This is the day of which men have
    dreamed;
For which scientists and astronauts
    have schemed.
A "take off" into the vast unknown
Where modern man is much alone.
First visit to the moon is now achieved,
But faith in God is still believed.
A solar adventure is "out of this world,"
But the moon now bears a flag
    unfurled.
The Sea of Tranquility is now known to
    man,
And the Ocean of Storms is next to be
    scanned.
Splash-Down, Re-Entry and a famous
    spacewalk
Now are terms to be used in every day
    talk.
Lunar Exploration is the future search
To delve into rock, rills and earth.
Will man find the answer to all outer
    space —
To the origin of earth and the human
    race?
May God grant that man may find
Knowledge to aid all mankind.

FRIENDSHIP
(1969)

It has been said the next man is your
    brother,
But most humans are selfish to each
    other.
Stewardship as the bible teaches
Is to use your talent to far reaches.
Results of a talent are meant to share;
The reward is showing others that you
    care.
A gentle word left unspoken
Adds to the grief of a heart that is
    broken.
To be alone is to despair;
Sorrow and love are meant to share.
Only those who have suffered loss
Are able to carry another's cross.
And those who live in an ivory tower
Seldom give aid or offer a flower.
Worldly wealth meets the need of
    pride,
But depart this life and it is laid aside.
That life that concerns only selfish
    needs
Is shallow and empty — the result of
    greed.
A friend who heeds the cry of lonely
    hearts
Reflects part of the joy he gladly
    imparts.
It is your aim to be a true friend
You must take care not to offend.
Most human hearts cannot conceive
It is much more blessed to give than
    receive.

Love is usually returned in due course;
Not always from those who receive,
    but some other source.
A kindness stemming from the heart
Joy to others does impart.
If you receive from a friend a treasure,
Give it quickly away to enjoy double
    measure.
The most joy in life with which to
    contend
Is to be able to say: "I have a friend."

LIFE'S GIFTS
(June, 1971)

Little things along life's way
Take the evil thoughts away.
Enjoy the rosey hues of dawn,
Chance of seeing a small spotted fawn.
Examine the minute parts of a flower;
God will grace it with a shower.
Hark to the chatter of a wee wren;
Think of the places he may have been.
Search the land, sea and air
For hidden gifts which God put there.
Treasure the hours of quiet peace,
When worry and tension seem to cease.
Look up to the distant stars in the sky;
Let your thoughts rise just as high.
Drift in the soft darkness of night,
Knowing God will put all things right.

H - E - L - P
(August, 1976)

H elp me to learn the way
E very day to make life pay.
L eaving undone if need be
P lease give some peace to me.

M ending hearts along the way
E ver mindful what You say.

G rant unto me thy love
O ver seas and skies above;
D own to earth may I be.

BEAUTIFUL DAY
(September, 1976)

The sun rose late this September day;
A summons, not to work, but to play.
One of those days when all goes well;
Balm to self, where the soul does dwell.
First to church to sing and to pray;
The very best way to start the day.
Then visit the home of a lonely friend
To shorten hours as the clock does
    bend.
Food, and drink and other Nature's gift,
All add up to give one a "lift".
Plans and dreams fall into place
And we feel love for the human race.
As the sun is on its way
We sigh and say, "What a beautiful
    day!"

LIGHTS AND SHADOWS
(August, 1976)

The changing shades of morning's light
Turns dark night-time into sunlight.
Early risers view a shade of plum;
Blue skies turned red by the rising sun.
Shadowy figures of gnarled trees
And strange forms in a misty breeze.
Creeping rays of sunlight bold
Light the awakening world with gold.
Dew drops on the dawn's wet grass
Sparkle like jewels of colored glass.
Tulips and roses and plantings rare;
Buds unfurl and the color's there.
After a storm there is rain washed air;
Then sunshine again and skies are fair.
The shelter of cool inviting shade;
Fresh, clear water — a nice place to
    wade.
Darkening storms may cloud the sky,
But twinkling stars are still near-by.
Shadows in the eerie twilight
Now proceed the dark of night.